Breathtaker

Breathtaker

By B. Hollis Knight

Dream Catcher Publishing, Inc.

Breathtaker

Copyright © 2004 by B. Hollis Knight.
All Rights reserved.
ISBN: 0-9720495-0-9 (Paperback)

Library of Congress Control Number 2003111523

Published by Dream Catcher Publishing Inc.

This book is a work of fiction. Places, events and situations in this story are purely fictional. Any resemblance to actual persons, living or dead is coincidental.

No part of this book may be reproduced, stored in a retrieval system or transmitted by any means, electronic, mechanical, photocopying, recording, or otherwise, without written permission from the author.

This book is printed on acid free paper

For information contact:

Dream Catcher Publishing, Inc.
P.O. Box 14058
Mexico Beach, Fl. 32410
Phone: 850-647-3637
Fax: 888-771-2800
Email: DCP@DreamCatcherPublishing.net

Breathtaker

Acknowledgements

There are so many people to thank for their encouragement to continue writing over the years. There is no way that I can remember everyone, so thank all of you very much.

I wish to thank the following people for their encouragement to continue writing and to complete this book.

My wife of 41 years, Grace Alene Nix Knight, my son Bryon Knight and especially my friend and published author: Dwan G. Hightower.

A special thank you to the following people for their efforts in getting the book ready for press.

Editing: Sabrina Gaskill, Robert Overstreet
Research: Grace Alene Nix Knight

Dedication

To my wife Grace

Introduction

It was late March and the early dawn would soon make way to the warm sun, bringing with it, the early breath of spring. Somewhere on the high slopes, a coyote lay just outside her den nursing her three young pups and five deer nipped cautiously on tender winter grass down near a creek at Rocky Point. The winter coats of the deer blended with the early shadows and the moss growing on the scrubby blackjack trees. It was quiet on brushy mountain as I leaned against a hollow log, enjoying my favorite time of day and trying to put a story together for a new book. I was totally in tune with nature and I listened to the peaceful sounds of the small stream a dozen feet away. The water gurgled as it meandered, trickling through the rocks, making its way down to the creek some eight hundred feet below. Now and again a faint breeze would blow through the brush and stir a few remaining dead leaves left from the fall shedding and a bald eagle flew from a lone dead tree, making plans to soar high somewhere above eastern Oklahoma's beautiful Lake Tenkiller, a place where peace and tranquility exist among secluded mountains and coves of quiet blue waters.

Suddenly the thought came to me and I knew what I wanted to do… I knew exactly what kind of book I wanted to write. I folded open my lap-top and begin to pound the key-board, writing about a man and his beautiful gray horse he had named ***Breathtaker.***

Chapter 1

    Jess Steel was a horseman all the way through to the bone and demonstrated the look by the clothes that he wore. He was a well-educated man but Jess was probably born 135 years too late, for he lived, ate, and breathed western history and ways of the old cowboys. He was a good rancher and everybody in the county knew it. Jess was known for his breeding of fine quarter horse racing stock and he loved the sport with all his heart. Every time you'd see Jess, he would be talking about his horses. Jess was always a sharp dresser and would be wearing a clean black western hat, a nice western shirt, starched jeans, good boots and he would be the same ole Jess Steel every time you met him. Jess always had a saying that if a man didn't have on good boots, belt and a good hat, well, he probably wasn't much of a rancher. Jess had just turned forty his last birthday but that didn't slow him down any. He was a 185-pound man just better than six feet tall and wide at the shoulders and narrow at the hips. He was as hard as steel and could still wrestle down the wildest and meanest calf in the pen come branding time. Jess always had a dark tan, probably assisted by his one-eighth Choctaw blood. He wore a well-groomed mustache that dropped down around the corners of his mouth, giving him the look of a true, old time, western cowboy. Even though Jess was as strong as an ox in a wiry sort of way, he was a gentle family man who knew the value of a true friends and Jess Steel possessed many.

Things have changed a lot over the years, wars have been fought, Presidents impeached by the house but not confirmed by the senate. A presidential election was determined by the U.S. Supreme Court and the people divided because of it. On a dark day in the year 2001 the twin towers fell due to vicious acts of fanatical terrorists. The people have united through fear, turning into strength and they seem to have rallied around the President. The war on terrorism is underway with no end in sight. Our leaders have now begun to expand the war and are looking toward Iraq once again and who knows, maybe for good reason. The country seems to have slipped back ten years and the economy has fallen into a state of recession with thousands out of work and the possibility of prosperity uncertain for many. Yes, political winds have definitely swayed the bushes. Even though we have seen a lot of change politically, there are some non-political things that have not changed and never will, especially things a horseman remembers that possess a special place in his heart.

It was just breaking gray light outside when Jess walked into the barn. He could hear the sounds of the twenty young two-year-old racing prospects bumping the stall gates and nudging feed buckets. The sounds echoed up and down the shed row. Now and again the sound of a muffled nicker could be heard, letting Jess know they were ready to eat. They were anticipating the tasty, sweet grain that came every morning at six o'clock. The birds that nested in the shed row were just coming off their roosts and greeting the new morning with their cheerful calls as they began their nest-building day.

The colts in the barn were the new two-year-old crop of quarter horse racing prospects that Jess and Susan Steel had raised the year before. Even though they were offspring of some of the finest stallions in the country and were bred to race, most wouldn't make it as race horses.

Most of the youngsters either wouldn't have the desire to run or the ability to run fast enough, or they would likely be plagued with injuries that would stop their racing careers before they began.

One of the colts born that year was a leggy, gray, stand-up kind of colt that stood out among the others. The colt had a personality that was a unique one. Jess was taken with this colt and believed the colt had it all. Jess believed he had the right ingredients to be a good racehorse. He knew that he had great athletic ability. He also knew the colt was a fighter, a survivor, and possessed that necessary ingredient called 'heart,' for he had proved that at his birth. Heart and the will to try would be essential if he were to ever become a class race horse

It has been several years now since Jess Steel told me the story about one such event but I remember it as though it were yesterday. Jess and Susan had been married for about fifteen years at that time and they loved each other better than life itself. They had built a new apartment in their barn for the purpose of keeping close check on the brood mares at foaling time. Jess had installed video cameras that were positioned toward the foaling stalls so that they could observe the brood mares. It was early, 3:00 a.m.., February second, 1985, when Jess awoke and the stall monitor mounted near the bedroom ceiling revealed activity in one of the sixteen-by-twenty-foot foaling stalls. It was time for their prize brood mare, "Ms. Gallant Lady," to foal. The long- awaited birth of her foal was now at hand. Jess sprang from the bed half asleep, quickly pulled on his jeans, not taking the time to tuck in the shirt. Susan sat up quickly in bed and through sleepy eyes looked at the monitor. Jess slipped on a boot and ran for the foaling stall carrying one boot and wearing the other. There was never much time when a mare finally lay down to deliver her foal. From previous year's experience Jess knew that every second counted if something were to go wrong. The powerful contractions of the mare would break the foal's neck if the head was not turned correctly in the birth canal. When Jess arrived at the foaling stall the mare was already down and the mighty contractions had begun. He quietly stepped inside the stall and stood watching her. Suddenly the mare's water broke, creating what seemed to be a small, equine Niagara Falls. The contractions were rapid now as the sleek, dark bay mare groaned and strained in effort to deliver. Suddenly a white membrane sack bubbled out. Quickly the foal's front feet began to emerge and they were in the correct position, one just ahead of the other and the bottoms of the little hooves pointing down toward the mother's back legs. The birth process continued with each heavy contraction and the foal moved slowly until the small nose appeared, but it was still inside the placenta. Jess quickly removed the membrane from around the little foal's nose. It appeared to be a normal birth and all that was needed now was the short wait for the final delivery. The mare would lie still for a minute and rest, then the powerful contractions and groans would continue. As the contractions became more severe and in an effort to push out the foal's front shoulders, she would raise her head and flex her neck back toward her flank area with her legs fully extended outward in order to gain leverage. The foal was now almost totally out and it lay motionless. Much of the little foal's body was still inside the placenta and showed no sign of movement. After a few seconds Jess realized that something was critically wrong. There was no movement. The foal lay motionless and Jess knew that it must draw its first breath. Suddenly he reached out and tore the membrane from the little foal. Jess began a rhythmic massage up and down the foal's body with both hands trying to stimulate him. There was still no movement, no sign of life. He hurriedly picked up a piece of straw and placing it inside the foal's nose and began to tickle the inside lining of the nose in an effort to cause the foal to sneeze and take breath. This trick had worked once in the past when a foal was in trouble, but not this time. Still nothing happened and the foal continued to lie still. Jess was near panic now and he frantically gathered up the limp foal in his arms. Jess clutched the foal's nose with his hands and placed its nose and mouth into his. He held him firmly between his legs and began to blow air into its lungs as hard as he could, then he would force the air to escape by pressing his knees to his sides and again blow into the lungs. This went on for what seemed to be an endless time, and then suddenly the foal drew its first breath, taking Jess's breath along with it and almost collapsing Jess's lungs in the process. Jess felt as though he had been punched in the pit of his stomach with someone's fist. The foal began to move now, trying to raise his unsteady little head. His head wobbled as he nickered softly as if to say, "hello, mom," or greet the new awaiting world. He was a beauty and a healthy specimen. Jess examined his feet and dipped the severed navel cord in iodine to kill any possible germs. The feet and legs were all normal. He had long pasterns and legs that no doubt would carry him across the finish line many times. Susan had eased up to the stall and stood smiling. She handed Jess a towel that she had brought with her. Jess dried the foal off and then Ms. Gallant Lady got up. The mare was covered with a light sweat and exhausted from the delivery. The mare turned facing the small foal and began to clean her baby as Jess and Susan both had seen brood mares do many times in the past. Jess quietly left the foaling stall to allow her to create a motherly bond with her new baby. The mare continued the process of nudging him, nickering quietly and persuading him get on his feet to nurse. This was always a process that required patience that only a mother could have with a new born. The foal suddenly tried to get on his feet and found that his unsteady, long legs would not hold him. He would try time and again, and then the little fellow would fall back to the stall floor that had been bedded with pine shavings, only to make another attempt. Finally he made it, stood on wobbly legs for a second, and then took his first step in an effort to reach the sweet smell of his mothers' warm, life-sustaining milk. He first tried locating the milk at the mare's front legs with no success. He frantically tried searching up and down both sides of the mare, unsuccessfully. He was really getting hungry now and after four or five minutes of searching, stomping and tail switching, he made the connection. He nursed rapidly, smacking as he began learning the nursing process. He swallowed in gulps, switching his little tail rapidly, consuming the wonderful food and necessary anti-bodies from the fresh colostrums. That first milk was essential. He must have it in order to survive and fight off germs and disease in his early life.

Jess and Susan stood watching the process and admiring the dark-colored foal that would no doubt be a dark gray when he shed his baby coat of hair. They began to think of possible names for the foal and instantly it came to them. The perfect name. . . "Breathtaker"! . . . That was it! They'd call him Breathtaker. Even though it was warm inside the foaling barn when he was born, that little fellow had surely taken Jess Steel's breath away on that cold frosty, February morning. Yes, Breathtaker was the perfect name.

Chapter 2

It had now been two weeks since the arrival of Breathtaker and he was a bundle of playful, unintentional mischief that was for sure. Jess would get to the barn early, before Alex Haygood, his trainer, arrived to begin the feeding chores, just for an opportunity to play with the foal in the peaceful quiet of the early morning. The little foal was a fool about scratching, especially at the root of his tail. When Jess would enter the stall and scratch him in his favorite spot, he would extend his neck backward toward his tail. He would stand on three legs with one back leg off the ground licking his tongue out and nibbling at Jess's arm or any other part he could find to bite. Jess would open the stall door and turn Breathtaker and Ms. Gallant Lady out into the shed row. That would give Jess an opportunity to play the foal's favorite game of 'hide and seek.' The mare would nibble on the bales of hay that Alex had stacked in front of each stall and ignore the foal for a while. Jess would hide behind the stacks of hay up and down the long shed row, and then he would call Breathtaker. Breathtaker would look in the direction of the voice, and then go running down the shed row in an effort to find him. Once he had located Jess, he would squeal, buck, and kick his heels up and race back to his mother as fast as his little legs would carry him. This would go on for at least half an hour every morning, and then Jess would put the pair back into the stall before Alex arrived. Somehow, it seemed a little silly for a grown man to be playing a child's game with a horse, but Jess could not help himself.

After a couple of months he had to quit playing with the foal so much. He was fast developing some really bad habits. Breathtaker would try and kick at Jess every time he entered the stall. Poor Alex had been kicked and bitten all over. Alex kept saying that Breathtaker had a mean streak, but Jess knew what was wrong. Jess had him just a little spoiled, that was the problem. Jess kept his mouth shut about playing with the foal so much.

Breathtaker's first summer was a season of exploration. He examined everything on the ranch and got into everything accessible. He played and raced across the pasture with the other foals that had been born that year. All of the foals would play until they were completely tired out. Then they would take long and frequent naps soaking up the sun and growing. . . Breathtaker was the fastest of them all and it was a pleasure to watch him run. Breathtaker ran with long easy strides and seemed to just float across the pasture when in full flight. Jess was really proud of this foal. After Alex finally stopped the biting and kicking habit that Jess had taught Breathtaker so well, Alex had taken a liking to Breathtaker and took every opportunity to show him off to his many racing buddies who came by the barn. Alex showed the brood mares and their offspring to every guest who came to the ranch that year and Breathtaker was the favorite of them all.

One time that summer, Alex and Jess were doing something in the shed row of the barn, I don't remember exactly what Jess said they were doing, but they kept hearing a muffled whinny coming from behind the barn. They didn't think too much about it for a few minutes, but then it continued. Jess walked to the back door and looked out into the pasture where the brood mares were all congregated quietly in the shade of a big elm tree escaping the mid-day heat. The mares and foals all stood stomping and swatting flies that were always a nuisance at that time of year. Jess didn't see anything alarming so he turned to go back inside, then the sound came again. This time Jess looked in the direction of the strange sound and there was Breathtaker standing next to the fence with his legs spread wide. "Alex! Take a look at this. Breathtaker is in one hell of a mess out here," said Jess, as he began to laugh.

Alex took a quick look and then ran to the tack room laughing. He grabbed up a pair of bolt cutters that he kept there for such emergencies.

"Come on, Jess, let's ease up to him. Then I'll try and get him out of that mess."

One of the plastic feed buckets that normally hung on the fence row had been relocated. Breathtaker had somehow managed to get the bucket loose from the fence and over his head. The bucket was secured by the bales and completely cut off his vision. Breathtaker stood extremely still and it was evident that he knew there was no escape from the contraption. He was just standing there nickering now and again, waiting for someone to come get the bucket off his head. Jess walked up to the foal slowly, talking to him as he approached. Jess reached out and began to scratch Breathtaker at his favorite spot while Alex took the bolt cutters and cut the bales off the bucket, setting him free. Breathtaker wheeled around, kicked up his heels and ran to his mother and began nursing as though he was completely starved. They both laughed and knew that he wasn't hungry. He just wanted some motherly reassurance.

Breathtaker was now five months old and had shed some of his baby hair and the gray velvety coat was evident on his head and lower legs. The gray color genes had been passed down by his gray, thoroughbred sire. Jess knew that he was going to be a good looking horse that was for sure. He had changed from a dark coat over his body to a silvery gray color that gave him the distinction of royalty and beauty.

It was time to wean the colts off their mothers so

Jess and Alex brought all of the mares and colts inside the barn and then stalled each mare and colt. Alex had halter broken all the colts when they were little and had them all broke to lead, so separating the mares from the little ones was a relatively easy task. The mares were turned out into the pasture and some of them hung around the gate leading into the main brood mare pasture for a day or so but most went on their way grazing. They actually seemed to be enjoying the freedom of not having to submit to their foals. The young horses in the barn were a different story, especially Breathtaker. He threw tantrums, stomped, kicked the wall, tried to climb the walls and anything else that a horse can do for about three days and nights. He wanted his momma and he wanted her then. He finally managed to settle down and act like he was a regular horse and the process was at last complete. Alex kept them up in the stalls for a few days. They all now had accepted the separation from their mothers so Alex began grooming and handling them on a regular basis. They didn't have momma anymore so they quickly become accustomed to the handling and enjoyed the human company. The sweet oats and vitamin supplement diet that Alex prepared for them twice a day was also one of their desires.

  Every time Alex would go into Breathtaker's stall he would come out talking about how the colt was growing or showing Jess a new bite mark. Alex began calling him a 'gray devil' and began his 'no-bite' schooling once again. Alex brought a big baked potato to the barn one morning and heated it in the microwave until it was hot through and through. He placed it into his shirt sleeve with a hand towel under it to avoid getting burned and entered Breathtaker's stall. Just as quickly as he entered, the colt began nibbling on him. Alex eased his arm toward the colt and Breathtaker suddenly took a big bite of the bulging sleeve containing the hot potato. The colt jumped backward and snorted and began chomping his teeth and shaking his head. That was the last time that he tried his biting tactics on anyone. The hot potato trick always seemed like a hard thing to do, but it was absolutely necessary and it worked every time on a chronic biter. Alex knew that when Breathtaker became a two-year-old, he would at some point have picked one them up by the arm and carried him out of the stall with his teeth. Alex knew that a young stallion needed some discipline while growing up. That wasn't the first time that Alex had dealt with a chronic biting problem and he knew that was the quickest and best way to handle the situation.

    The colts were all turned out for the rest of the summer and allowed to run and grow strong. Breathtaker continued to build muscle and look the part of a grown horse until he reached the yearling stage. The second summer was filled with daily wrestling, biting and adolescent horseplay. It was the stage in a young horse's life when he becomes rough looking and odd shaped. Some parts seem to outgrow the others. This stage always produces a ragged look that slowly goes away at about sixteen months. At that age they become sleek and beautiful specimens and Breathtaker was no exception.

Chapter 3

It was early spring and sparrows frantically fluttered about, littering the shed row with straw from their busy days of nest building. Jess looked at his watch and it was now seven-thirty. All of the horses had completed eating and the day's work was ready to begin. Alex removed a halter and lead from just outside Breathtaker's stall, opened the stall door and stepped inside. Alex Haygood had been working for Jess Steel for almost five years. He was a top trainer and a seasoned hand with horses. Alex always talked to the young horses as he handled them. Alex slid his hand down the soft, velvety neck of the big, silver-gray colt and then slipped the halter over Breathtaker's nose and buckled it over the head. "It's stall cleaning time, big boy. It's time for you to walk the circle." Alex snapped the lead rope into the bottom ring of the halter and led Breathtaker out to the walker.

Alex always said the same thing to the colts every time he put them on the hot walker. It seemed as though they each knew what was about to happen from his conversations with them and I guess they probably did.

Alex Haygood was a former professional jockey who had unfortunately experienced leg problems that had forced him to quit riding in races for a living. He walked with a slight limp from a spill experienced sometime in the past, but he was a good hand with a horse, probably the best Jess Steel had ever seen. Even though he could no longer race as a professional jockey, he still did all of the exercising of the colts each morning. He would ride a colt, bathe him and put him on the hot walker while the stable boy cleaned the stall and provided fresh bedding. Alex would leave them on the walker until they were completely dry. Then he would groom them and put them back in the clean, freshly bedded stall.

Breathtaker was now eighteen months old and Alex knew the time had come to begin breaking him to ride. Alex lifted the bridle with the D-ring snaffle bit off the hook and headed to Breathtaker's stall. He eased the bit into the colt's mouth and craftily pulled it over the colt's ears. Breathtaker didn't like the bit at all. He chomped the bit vigorously with his teeth as though he wanted to bite it in half, but to no avail. The bit was there to stay so he wore it almost all that day before Alex returned to the stall with a halter and an old breaking saddle. By this time, Breathtaker had accepted the bit and stopped the chomping. Alex entered the stall, slipped the halter on over the bridle and securely tied Breathtaker up tight to the heavy stall gate post. Alex gently stroked the colt on the neck and continued talking to him for a few minutes to settle him down. Once this process was completed Alex eased the saddle pad over onto Breathtaker's back. The process of pulling the pad off and replacing it on his back continued for five or ten minutes until he became accustomed to the pad. Alex slowly picked up the saddle and eased the stirrup fender over Breathtaker's back and settled it firmly in place. Breathtaker stood still but Alex could see the signs of nervousness in Breathtaker's eyes. Jess reached under Breathtaker's stomach and took hold of the girth and pulled the cinch strap through the buckle ring barely snug. Alex continued petting and talking to the colt and after a few minutes Alex took a second loop in the cinch and pulled it fairly tight and then quickly buckled it snugly in place. Breathtaker shied and pranced nervously, humped his back and stood wide eyed for a few minutes before finally relaxing. Jess let Breathtaker stand in the stall wearing the saddle the remaining part of the day before removing it. The next two days were days of wearing the saddle and Breathtaker had finally accepted it and acted as though he didn't notice it being on his back at all. On the fourth day, Alex closed the sliding doors at each end of the hallway, saddled the colt and led him out of the stall. He snapped a pair of cotton driving lines onto the D-ring bit then ran a line through each of the saddle stirrups. After about a week of this driving, Jess saddled Breathtaker and left him in the stall. He took a loop around the gate post and held the end of the lead rope in his left hand. Jess eased his foot into the stirrup and, keeping the rope tight, forced the colt's nose to be snug against the post. He slowly swung his leg over the saddle and was mounted. He sat talking to the colt for a few minutes before slowly dismounting. This process went on for a couple of days until Breathtaker accepted the weight of someone being on his back. On the third morning Jess mounted and slowly eased the rope from around the post allowing the colt to walk around in the 12' X 12' stall for a while. This process was continued for a couple of days until the morning Jess reached down and opened the stall gate and allowed Breathtaker to step out into the hallway. Breathtaker walked to the end of the hall as though he had been ridden for three months. Jess rode him in the hallway every day, teaching him to stop, and handling him enough to keep control of his head when they went to the track the first time. Breathtaker took to the riding just like an old horse.

    Every time Alex took Breathtaker to the exercise track he would come back bragging on that colt. The gray colt always seemed to give a little more than he was asked, every time he'd take him out to work. Even though Jess was the owner of the horses, he took no active part in the training. He knew that Alex was a professional and depended on Alex's expertise. He also knew that

Breathtaker was a special colt. He spent too much time at the barn grooming and fooling with Breathtaker not to know that. After all, he literally breathed the breath of life into him when he was born. The colt and Jess formed a special kind of bond. A bond and a trust that a horseman often has and develops with a beautiful colt that's a fighter, especially one that he feels is going to be great someday. That bond is a lifetime experience that always stays in a horseman's mind even after the short life of his great horse may have expired.

Alex hunkered at Breathtaker's front legs, working feverishly applying the leg wraps. Alex suddenly looked up at Jess. "Jess, I've asked Mike to come by the barn early every morning help me for a while. He` will come early before he goes to the track to exercise horses. I want to work Breathtaker with another horse for a few days. He needs to be worked some before the schooling race next week anyway."

"You're the trainer, Alex. That sounds good to me and speaking of Mike, here he comes now."

Mike strolled into the barn carrying his exercise saddle. "Good morning!" said Mike, as he stopped, sizing Breathtaker up for a second.

"Mike, catch that horse in the third stall on the left and let's work him with Breathtaker this morning. He sprints out pretty well and he needs the exercise."

Mike led the horse out into the shed row and began grooming him. "What's the plan this morning, Alex?"

"We're just going to work them together and let them sprint out for about a lap and a half. I want you to take the lead, ah, say maybe three or four lengths, then I'll push Breathtaker a little and let him catch up to your horse and pass him. I want him to pass your horse up and run about a length out front, just enough so that he can hear your horse behind him. We'll do this a few days and see what happens. I want Breathtaker to get it in his head that he can pass anything that is in front of him. We'll keep pushing then each day a little until he gets the hang of it."

"I guess that's what separates the good trainers from the bad ones. Boy, you don't miss a trick training Jess's colts. Most of those boys training out there at the track don't ever work their colts with another horse until they go to the track for a schooling race."

Alex looked up at Mike and smiled. "Well, Mike, the difference in their kind of training and mine is simple. We don't get any day money for training from some out-of-state owner. Most of them just hang a horse on a walker for an hour a day and keep him groomed and looking pretty and then put the poor colt in a race and he can't run because he's not in shape and that ain't training in my book. Out here, we actually try to train a colt to win a race. Some of those 'so called trainers' you're talking about don't care whether a colt wins or not. They've got twenty five or thirty head of horses in their barn that they are supposed to be training and that times thirty-five dollars a day is a lot of money they're taking in every thirty days. Ole Jess and me, you see, we don't have any day money coming unless it's the day of the race and we win. That's what I call 'need more money' and I sure need more."

For the next five days, they worked the horses together and by this time Breathtaker had figured out that he was supposed to out run the other horse. When Alex would call on him, Breathtaker would blow by Mike's horse as though he was not running.

It was a cool morning and Jess looked at his watch. It was 7:30 and the sixth day of working the horses together. Mike came strolling into the barn with sleepy eyes. "Alex, this daylight savings time is getting to me," said Mike, as he laid his saddle down on a bale of hay.

Jess looked at Mike and laughed. "Well, Mike, we're going to see if we've done any good this morning. Get that bay three-year-old horse out of stall seven. We'll let them burn for a couple hundred yards this morning and see what happens."

Mike smiled. "Can that bay run some?

He can run a bunch. He's got a 97 speed index and run out a little over $33,000.00 last year as a two-year-old," said Alex.

As they rode out onto the training track, Alex looked at Mike and pointed to the far turn.

"We'll take them around once and let them loosen up. When we get to that turn, turn him loose and let him run for about a hundred yards. Better than that, let him make the hook and run all the way down the back stretch before you pull him up," said Jess.

As they approached the turn, Alex took a deep seat and told Mike to turn the bay loose. The big bay colt lunged hard, getting a full length on Breathtaker, and then Alex slapped Breathtaker on the neck and called on him. Breathtaker pinned his ears and went after the bay up ahead. The bay was kicking up dirt on Breathtaker but he paid no attention to the dirt flying all over him. He was headed for the horse ahead and trying to catch him. Alex called on the gray colt once more and Breathtaker responded with a burst of speed putting him nose to nose with the bay speedster. When they came out of the turn into the stretch, Mike sat down and went to work with his crop calling on the bay for all he had. Alex slapped Breathtaker lightly on the neck once again then began to talk to him. "Come on, colt, take him, come on, come, boy" Breathtaker seemed to get lower, stretching his stride, and then suddenly Breathtaker gave that extra effort Alex was looking for. Two strides carried him on by the bay, putting him a full length ahead at the end of the stretch. Mike stood up on the bay and Alex began to slow Breathtaker. As they reached the lane leading up to the barn, Mike had a big smile on his face. Jess climbed down from the fence where he had been watching and met them.

"Jess! You've got you a runner! Don't you think Alex?"

Jess slapped Mike on the shoulder. "That was some race. At first I didn't think Breathtaker could take the bay. I don't know what you did to make him blow by him like that, Alex, but he did it real easy like," said Jess, with a big, wide smile on his face.

"I've been telling y'all this gray devil could fly!" Alex jumped down from Breathtaker's back and led him on toward the barn as they talked about the race.

It had been a week now since Breathtaker won his official schooling race at the track by an easy seven lengths, and both Alex and Jess were excited about their chances in the up-coming futurity. Alex had completed the morning work at the barn and came walking down the hallway and sat down in a lawn chair where Jess sat reading a racing magazine.

"Well, Jess, now we know about how good Breathtaker really is, since winning the schooling races last week. I've been thinking about it a lot. The 'Black Gold Futurity Trials' are next week and they ain't going to be like that schooling race, that's for sure. I know one thing. He's up against some of the best futurity colts in the country," said Alex as he wiped his face with a towel.

Jess closed the magazine and noticed that Alex was looking straight at him as though waiting for confirmation.

"We've got some top competition, that's for sure. He may not win the heat race but somehow, I've got a gut feeling that Breathtaker will run up front. Alex, he may not win the race but he'll be in there."

Alex meditated on what Jess had just said for a moment, knowing that just being in there, and running up front wasn't good enough. He picked up a bridle lying just inside the tack room door and began examining it nervously.

"Yes, sir, I think he'll do all right *if* he gets out of

the gate quick enough. I just don't want him to get the idea that he can't pass the horse in front of him. I believe that makes the difference in how a horse will try in the future."

"Alex, I don't think that it would matter if Breathtaker didn't get out of the gate quick enough. That colt will always try, that you can be assured of. But of course, we don't want that to happen"

Alex nodded his head in agreement, looked down the shed row toward the colts stall, then added; "I heard talk yesterday about that 'Dash for Cash' colt that's here from the west coast. They say that he's been clocked running "AAA" time already, un-officially, that is. To me that's dangerous to put that much pressure on a young colt that has open knees not fully developed, when there is nothing at stake," said Alex.

"Alex, I guess everybody is guilty of that. You just let Breathtaker take his time; make his own way when he runs. Just tell the boy that's up next week to just set down on him and ride. Breathtaker will run with them without even calling on him, I expect."

Alex got up from where he was sitting and walked down the hallway toward Breathtaker's stall. As he passed the stall, he stopped and leaned against the stall door and studied the colt for a minute before continuing on down the shed row. Jess watched the small- framed man as he walked out of the barn and couldn't help but wonder if Alex was enjoying training as much as he did working as a jockey. Alex was now fast approaching forty-five years old and had begun to gray some in the temples. His tobacco-stained mustache also showed signs of graying. The heavy age lines in the little man's face showed evidence that he had obviously lived a hard life while earning the good money as one of the leading jockeys in the country. Alex had been extremely successful in his career and had won the prestigious "All American Futurity" at Ruidoso Downs in New Mexico several years back. Successful or not, he didn't have much to show for it. He was forced to retire practically broke due to fast living but somehow he had managed to pay for eighty acres of land that had a small rock house on it that he lived in. Alex never talked about his life as a jockey or races that he had won. Once in a while he would use the name of a good horse he had ridden as a comparison to Breathtaker's ability. He sure enough did like that gray colt. It was almost as if he believed Breathtaker was his way back to the good times, and it was Jess's guess that he would be, if the colt could run with the best of them.

As a new day began, Alex entered Breathtaker's stall in his usual talkative manner.

"Well, today, big boy, this is the day you are going to learn to break out of the starting gate like a race horse should. I reckon it can be easy or it can be hard but I dreamed about it last night and it wasn't good. You must learn to get your big, gray rear end out of that gate and do it quickly if you are going to run with the best."

Alex secured the small pancake saddle on Breathtaker and then swung up on his back. As they rode out of the barn and turned out onto the training track he nudged the colt into a short canter. As he did, the big colt dropped his nose and arched the neck and began to pull against the bit. Alex began to talk to him with a quiet determined voice.

"That's the way, colt, pull on that bit hard. Feeling frisky, are you? Well, just you wait, you big gray devil, there's a nice purse just waiting out there for us and we want it, don't we, boy?"

Jess had already gone to the four-horse starting gate to watch as he usually did. He wouldn't have missed watching Breathtaker for the world. As he sat waiting for Alex to bring the colt around the track, he remembered when Breathtaker was a little fellow how he'd play hide and seek in the shed row. He remembered how he would hide and call Breathtaker and how Breathtaker would look behind each stack of hay trying to find him. He was the most curious colt Jess had ever seen and I guess that's why Jess came to love the colt so much. As they rounded the turn and approached the starting gate Jess could tell from where he was positioned near the starting gate that there was a certain determination in the little trainer's face like he had not seen before. Alex called out to Jess. "Hey, Jess! Will you pull the gates for me? We're going to teach this boy to get out fast this morning!"

Jess took one look at the gray speedster and nodded. Alex eased the colt into the starting gate. Then Jess closed the door behind him.

"Now, Jess, when I count to three, you pull the spring pin. We're coming out like a blue streak,"

Alex pulled his cap down tight and positioned himself just as though he were riding in a real race. Breathtaker stood nervously awaiting what was about to happen. He crouched down ready to lunge. Alex began the count slowly. "One. . . Two. . . Three . . . At the same instant the gate flew open, Alex screamed as loud as he could and brought a flat wide leather strap down on the haunches of the colt that popped loudly but caused little or no pain. Just as suddenly as the gate flew open, the dust boiled and Alex's rear end hit the ground with a thud. Breathtaker ran completely out from under Alex in one lunge and continued on down the track with his tail flowing in the breeze.

Alex looked up at Jess with a wide grin on his face and fighting the dust with both hands. "Holy smoke, Jess, he doesn't need any more teaching. He's ready to go now! He just needs a rider, that's all. He just needs a rider with two good leg. Jess, that's the hardest breaking colt I ever set my ass on. Man alive . . . Jess, I have rode a lot of horses in my life and I do believe we've got us a race horse!"

Chapter 4

As the spring sun warmed the earth, morning rays of light extended through a small cloud and gave the impression that the streams of light were attaching themselves to some distant point somewhere in eastern Oklahoma. The warm spring rains had come, but there was a light chill in the air. With the early spring rains, jonquils and tulips had sprung forth in abundance, creating a floral cascade of color around the newly constructed Blue Ribbon Downs race track in Sallisaw, Oklahoma. The quarter-mile-long parking lot across the track was filled with cars, trucks, and motor homes from several surrounding states. The shuttle buses were busy carrying racing fans to the grandstands for the day of racing. It would be an exciting day of qualifying trials for the big race. Today, Jess would know who the top ten contenders would be in the 'Black Gold Futurity.' Racing forms and scratch sheets were being sold just inside the gate of the state's largest quarter horse racing facility. There were colts from all over the country, some of the best. There was an R. Smith colt owned and trained by one of the leading local horseman. There were Kitterman bred colts trained by another top local trainer. There were two or three Bugs Alive colts from one of the major breeders in the state. Several horses were sons and daughters of the great horse, "Dash for Cash," that belonged to various owners across the country. There was also a gray colt called Breathtaker. He was out of 'Raise a

Lady' by "Raise your glass," by the great Kentucky Derby Winner, "Native Dancer." The big gray colt was trained by none other than Alex Haygood. Yes, Breathtaker was competing with the elite, some of the best in the world. The ten heats of the finals would produce the ten trial winners that would run in the finals for the rich 'Black Gold' purse.

Some of the young horses would likely break down that very day and have to be put down. Some others would possibly become cripples for perhaps a life time and maybe later have to be destroyed, while some would show prospect or perhaps prove their ability to run with the best. It was never a pleasant thought, but it was definitely a problem every owner and trainer in the quarter-horse-racing industry had to deal with. Unlike the thoroughbreds, quarter horses are allowed to race at two years old. They were all young, with immature knees that would not mature until their third year. There were some that could not stand up to the strain of their own powerful, exploding muscle. They would actually run so hard they would hurt themselves in many cases. It was a problem and today definitely would be a day of reckoning. It was the day that would determine the winner in each of the ten heat races securing each horse a spot in the finals and provide the owners a possible return on their Futurity investments, if they were lucky.

It was now ten A.M. and the upcoming post time of one o'clock was fast approaching.
Alex swung the Ford diesel pickup pulling the horse trailer into the trainer's gate and was motioned in by the guard. Breathtaker stood quietly as they rode on down the gravel drive to the haul-in barn. Alex opened the door of the horse trailer and the gray colt stepped out. He is a beautiful horse, thought Alex. Breathtaker raised his head high and stood proud. He looked all around as if to say:

"So this is what it's all about."

He was covered with a soft, rose-colored cooler that

Susan had made. The cooler was fancy and displayed black monogram letters, advertising Jess and Susan's Quarter Horse Ranch. Breathtaker held his head high, looking around as Alex led him into the barn.

Breathtaker was in the third race and Alex had drawn the number three position or 'three hole' as is common language in racing circles. The horse in the inside position, next to the rail, was the favorite in the race. He was that west coast colt that had been un-officially clocked at "AAA" time. Alex knew this could be a problem if the jockey knew to pull him tight against the rail. There was a narrow hard pan of soil that the harrow never quite tills that would give a horse better footing and allow him to run faster. The number two horse was an R. Smith Colt, which had a lot of local publicity and was expected to do well in the finals.

As post time came for the first race, the trumpeter played the familiar call of 'boots and saddles.' Breathtaker was standing in his stall quietly as the sound of the trumpet broke the still, crisp spring air. Suddenly Breathtaker raised his head high. He twitched one of his dark gray fox ears backward, listening to the strange sounds of the trumpet. That was something new to him. This was a sound that he would hear many times in the future, if he was lucky that day..

It was now time for the third elimination race and there could only be one winner. The ten speedsters reacted nervously in the saddling paddock. This was it, thought Alex, as he firmly held Breathtaker after he had just finished saddling him. The number one horse was a long, lanky sorrel that chewed frantically at the bit and became almost uncontrollable. His body was covered with a light sweat, seemingly anxious to turn on the afterburner for the three hundred and fifty yard race. Number two was the R. Smith colt and he too was ready to run. He pranced from side to side as the trainer held him tightly. Breathtaker stood quietly, but make no mistake, he was very alert. He seemed to be looking around at the large crowd of spectators that had gathered for a last minute view of the horses. He had a look about him that seemed to give one the impression that running with the best was no big deal. Number four was a solid black, son of Dash for Cash. He was nervously sweating and chomping his bit. He kicked and reared while the saddle was being secured. The number five horse was a red roan colt that continued to kick with one back foot as if he were planning to take out a part of the block wall behind him. The number six horse was a racy looking palomino-colored colt that had come in from the west coast and he, too, was a spectacular specimen of a race horse. He pranced and stomped his feet nervously as he chewed the D-ring bit and frothed at the mouth. The number seven and eight horses were almost a matched pair. Both were blood bays that demonstrated racy lines of quality breeding. They too were ready to race. Number nine was a dun colored colt that was rather small for a race horse, but extremely muscular. He demonstrated a powerful rear end and wide chest and Jess knew that he would break fast and sprint well. He was calm but knew that action was about to begin. The last colt was number ten, a big, black colt that was already frothing with white perspiration across his neck and shoulders from nervous excitement. Then the call came. Alex hoisted the jockey into the small pancake saddle and then the jockey asked for last minute instruction.

"Jackie, if I were up on this gray devil today, I'd take me a deep seat, hold on tight and scream at him as the gate opens. He'll break really hard. If you can keep your seat, just sit down on him, let him run, then you just ride this racehorse all the way to the wire. This gray colt can really run."

Breathtaker stepped lightly as they headed onto the track. He seemed to have a look of certain determination and confidence to handle the job at hand. Jess had seen that determination in him all of the colt's young life, from the time he drew that first breath until that very moment. Breathtaker pranced candidly as they paraded by the grandstand. He was a looker all right, with his nostrils flaring and his jet black mane and tail flowing in the spring breeze. His silvery gray coat was slick and soft to the touch from the long hours of grooming by Alex's brush. The jockey nudged him forward into a canter as the colorful bay and white paint pony horse bounced in short strides beside him. Breathtaker seemed to be floating along. His head was tucked as he pulled lightly on the bit.

Susan suddenly noticed that Jess had twisted the racing form that he had bought until it was ragged all over, in a state of nervousness that an owner gets just before a big race. After all, he had waited two years to find out if Breathtaker was worthy of being in the top ten. That time had come and Jess was sure to know soon. It would take less than twenty seconds to find out.

As they made the loop around the track, they were now within short distance of the starting gates. Breathtaker flicked his ears forward and shied a little to the left in anticipation of the quick action and noise that was sure to develop as the starting gates flew open. The one horse walked nervously into the gate and was fastened in. The second horse went easily into the number two stall. Breathtaker seemed to know what he must do as he quickly stepped into the number three stall and stood quietly. The number four and five horses eased into their stalls. The number six horse stepped inside his stall then suddenly ran backward breaking loose from the handler. After a moment they caught him and tried to get him into the gate once again and this time with success. Horses number seven and eight cautiously moved into their stalls. The number ten horse balked at entering. Then with some reassurance from the jockey, he stepped inside and the gate was latched behind him. Jackie Stone, Breathtaker's jockey, remembered what Alex had told him and sat down low on the horse, holding the reins tight along with a rather large hunk of Breathtaker's mane. Breathtaker seemed to crouch down ready to spring. Suddenly the number seven horse reared and flipped in the stall banging his head against the wall of the stall. As Jess watched through his binoculars, he knew from past experience that banging the head would be a problem. A horse would seldom run well if the horse was experiencing any pain and banging the head usually resulted in defeat. Now there were only eight horses for Breathtaker to contend with. The one horse lunged against the gate in an effort to make a false start. Now they were all standing still. It was a brief stillness, but dead silence that seemed to be a full minute. Then suddenly the bell went off and the gates flew open. Ten jockeys screamed all at once. Breathtaker lunged hard and lost his front footing in the soft track just outside the gate, almost going down. The jockey picked his head up and pointed him toward the finish line. Breathtaker seemed to know that he had lost valuable time and that the one horse was now a half length ahead. The jockey laid his right hand flat against the colt's neck and slapped him sharply, in an effort to reassure and stimulate the young horse. Breathtaker pinned his ears flat against his head and responded with a burst of speed that moved him in front by a nose. The one, two, and three horses were now running neck and neck with not more than six inches separating the lead. Then the announcer's voice rang clearly.

"Its number three now, It's Breathtaker in the lead. . . Number one and number two running hard, neck to neck but, they're still in there ladies and gentlemen. It's 'pocket full of money' making up ground on the outside, look at them run ladies and gentlemen, look - at - them - run! It's a real horse race . . . Now its Breathtaker still holding the lead by a nose as the three battle for the lead."

They were now within one hundred yards of the

finish line and Breathtaker was running easily, but not pulling away from the two spirited, speedsters at his left side. The jockey again laid his hand on the colt's neck and slapped him sharply, asking for more, and then the jockey began talking to him,

"Come on, boy, you can do it! Come on! Come on!" urged the small jockey as they bolted down the straight away track.

The gray colt seemed to remember Alex talking to him and suddenly responded, giving it his all. In two strides Breathtaker separated the two top contenders by a half length and was now running at full speed and in another gear that would be unmatched that day. As they swept under the finish wire the call of the announcers voice rang out clearly;

"It's Breathtaker by a length . . . what a horse race folks . . . what - a -horse - race!"

The crowd roared and Jess threw the remaining part of that racing form into the air along with his new felt hat. In excitement, Jess pulled Susan to him and squeezed her tight.

"Come on, girl, let's go to the winners circle," shouted Jess as they and ran toward the winners circle to get in the picture. No one was sure what became of Jess's new hat but someone must have enjoyed wearing it. Jess just hoped it brought him good luck for that was his lucky day. Jess knew then that Breathtaker was one of the top ten finalists and one of the best young race horses in the country.

Chapter 5

It had been two weeks since the trials and it was a sunny Saturday morning. It was the morning of the rich Black Gold finals and as Alex walked into the barn that morning he walked straight to Breathtaker's stall to check on him before starting with the chores. As he walked up to the stall a cold chill ran up and down Alex's back as panic began to set in.

"He's gone . . . He's gone! . . . The colt is gone," shouted Alex.

Alex ran as fast as he could to the telephone mounted in the shed row and dialed the Sheriff's department to report what had happened.

"My God, I need to call Jess," said Alex, as he breathed heavily.

When the telephone rang that morning Jess Steel never felt so sick in his life. He felt instantly angry and wanted to tear someone apart. Jess felt helpless, disappointed and just plain mad. He didn't care about the race; he just wanted his horse back. Jess wouldn't have traded him for ten Black Gold purses. He was his horse and no one had the right to steal him. Not knowing that Alex had already reported the problem to the Sheriff's office, Jess instantly called the Sheriff's office and notified them the second time.

I know the deputy that took the call thought Jess was crazy, but he was emotionally overcome by the news.

"I'm offering a five thousand dollar reward for the arrest and conviction of the person involved in taking my horse," he said, as he slowly laid the receiver down.

Suddenly cold fear gripped Jess as he thought about where Breathtaker might be headed. Jess knew that there were those in the country who would send him to the slaughter house for the sixty-cent-per-pound price being paid for killer horses. They didn't care what he was or if he was a race horse or for anything else. They just concerned themselves with what he weighed and the small sum that he would bring them per pound to cut his head off at the slaughter house for some Frenchman to enjoy eating.

It had now been five weeks since Breathtaker disappeared and during this time Jess and Alex had gotten but little work done around the barn. There was a lot of conversation and speculation as to what had actually happened to Breathtaker. Jess had made calls every day to the sheriff's office in hopes of good news but was fast giving up on any possibility of finding his horse. The sheriff's office added little hope and with an all-points bulletin out across the country, nothing had turned up. Jess was sure someone was holding him in the area until the heat was off and attempts of finding him were exhausted. Then it flashed through his mind that maybe they had plans to return him. Maybe for ransom. Jess knew that wasn't right, he didn't have much money. Every thing that he had was secured by the bank or tied up in his horses. After Jess thought about it for a minute, he realized that probably was not the case. After all, the big race was over now and they couldn't race him in a sanctioned race anyway because his registration papers were filed in the track office. If he had been taken early in the evening, shortly after feeding time, that would have given the thief a twelve-hour start and he could have possibly have made it across the border into Canada or Mexico. Jess was sick with worry and had eaten but very little since Breathtaker disappeared.

Alex walked up to where Jess stood leaning against a paddock fence watching a new foal run and play. He stood silent for a minute, nervously shifting his weight from side to side. "Jess, they're not going to find him, are they?"

"I don't know Alex. It sure doesn't look much like it. It's been thirty-five days now and it don't look so good to the sheriff's department. I don't know what else to do but just wait and hope something turns up," Jess said, as he scraped the ground with his right boot in frustration. "Did you hear that Alex?"

"Hear what?"

"That's the telephone in the barn!" shouted Jess. "Maybe there's word," Jess dashed for the barn and jerked the phone off the receiver. "Hello!" Then Jess heard the voice at the other end.

"Mr. Steel, this is Captain Tucker with the New Mexico State Police. I understand that you lost a gray racehorse recently."

"Yes, sir, I sure did. Five weeks ago. Did you find him?"

" I'm sorry to say, we didn't, but we received a call from the U.S. Border Patrol telling us that they had detained two Mexicans near El Paso for two or three days until they could get proper veterinary certified health papers on a horse so that they could cross the border. It seems as though they had some problem with the necessary paper work."

"What color was the horse?"

"They said the horse was a gray stallion. The Border Patrol didn't have the published bulletin at that time and they let him slip through," stated the Captain.

"Did the Mexicans have a bill of sale?"

"Yes, they said the bill of sale was written by some man by the name of Williams."

"They undoubtedly forged a bill of sale," said Jess.

"That's what we think too."

"Where do we go from here?"

"Well, we don't have any jurisdiction past the border and assistance from the Mexican police has not been anything to speak about in the past. We've already made contact with them but received a half-hearted promise to assist in the search."

"Well, let me ask you this, can I go down there and do my own investigation and look for my horse?"

"Oh, yes. You can. But, I would not advise it. The Mexicans are not likely to tell you much of anything even if you get a lead."

"All I want to know is where they crossed the border."

"At El Paso and right into Juarez. God knows which direction they took after they crossed the border. They could have gone any direction," said the Captain.

"Well, I sure appreciate the call, that's a lot more then we've heard since the horse disappeared," said Jess, as he hung up the telephone.

In a state of confusion, Jess quickly told Alex what he had learned from the police.

"What are you going to do, Jess?"

"Well, as quickly as I can pack some things, I'm going to take a trip to Mexico and look for my horse."

Alex cast a questionable look out of the corner of his eye. "I'll be ready in twenty minutes."

"Alex, I know you want to be a part of this, and believe me I know how you feel but we've got the other colts that need your attention. I may be able to do better own my own," said Jess as he watched Alex's face grow cold with disappointment.

"I know how you feel, but if he's there I'll bring him back, Alex. I may be gone for quite a spell, but I'll bring him back if it is at all possible."

"But Jess, I sure would like to go help look for

him," said Alex, as he almost pleaded with him.

That was the first time that Jess had ever known the little trainer to question his direction or plead for anything and it hurt to tell him no, but he had to. He had to do this alone.

Jess backed the Ford diesel pickup next to the three-horse slant trailer, and then the two of them quickly hooked it up.

As Jess walked into the house, he met Susan and she knew that something was up. "What are you about to do, Jess?" Susan stood staring questioningly at him with her pretty, dark eyes. Susan was a tall shapely woman with a well boned face. Her Cherokee blood from her grandmother's side of her family accounted for her dark features and smooth skin. She is a looker, thought Jess. Susan stared straight into his eyes. "What's up?"

She knew Jess like a book and as Jess gradually broke the news, he chose every word carefully as he laid out his plan to go look for Breathtaker.

"Jess Steel, I've lived with you for almost fifteen years and I have a bad feeling about you going off down there by yourself. What if you get killed or wind up in some Mexican jail or something?" she sharply stated.

Jess hesitated a little. "Well, Susan, I know how you feel but I've got to go look. I will never be satisfied if I don't look for him. Susan, you know how special this colt is to you and me both, and I don't think you would actually want it any other way if there is a chance of me finding him."

Susan dropped her head and began to cry.

"I know, Jess, but I'll worry about you the entire time you're gone," she said, as she wiped her eyes on the red checkered apron she was wearing.

"I know I'm wasting my time talking to you. You are as stubborn as a jack ass. I know you are not going to have it any other way. Jess, you must promise me that you will be extremely careful and that you'll stay in contact with me on a regular basis," she said, as she began to look for the black over-night bag that she kept in the bedroom closet.

"I'm already packed, Susan. I did that several days ago," said Jess.

"Sneaky, aren't you? I should have guessed."

"I promise that I'll stay in contact with you as much as I can and I'll be careful," said Jess as he quickly reached into the top dresser drawer and slipped his twenty-five automatic boot gun into his vest pocket.

"Alex is going to stay here and take care of things. If there is anything that you need for him to do just call the barn and he will help you."

As Susan finished packing his things, Jess drew her close and kissed her for a long time.

Forcing a smile, Susan looked at Jess. "You be extra careful down there. You will, won't you?"

"I will."

Jess knew that she was not happy about him taking off on a horse chase like that, but she knew that he had to. Jess quickly grabbed the bag and headed for the door.

"Bye. I'll call you every chance I get. Bye and I'll be careful. Don't worry, now."

As he started out the back door, Susan caught him by the back of his shirt and spun him around. She drew him close and kissed him hard and long.

"You keep your business straight Buster. There are some loose Señoritas down there, so you just mind your business and keep your pants pulled high."

He smiled at her as he quickly headed for the red Ford diesel pickup that he had left with the engine running.

She waved good-bye as he sped away toward Interstate Forty.

As he pulled onto Interstate Forty, Jess set the speedometer on eighty and locked it in. He knew he was speeding but he also knew that while he was driving, the thieves were making tracks somewhere in Mexico and every minute counted.

Chapter 6

It was just breaking daylight when Jess Steel dropped off highway 70 and took the high slope onto the desert near Tularosa, New Mexico, and headed south on highway 54. In the distance off to his right he could see the White Sands Missile Range and the hazy, jagged, blue Organ Mountain Range that lay beyond. The white sand seemed to be an endless, shivering sea that gave the visual impression of water. Miles of water, yet it was not water but heat being reflected from the hot white desert sand. The silvery streak extended across the floor of the desert to the base of the mountains beyond. There wasn't much out there to look at, but it had a special strange kind beauty like Jess had not seen before. Many of the desert cacti were blooming and purple sage dotted the desert floor. There were low-growing mesquite, Spanish bayonet and various kinds of cactus. As the truck rolled on in the early morning stillness, now and again Jess would spot a lone cow grazing on whatever she could find in the desert. It appeared to be an endless sea of low dunes each dotted with the purple sage. The only sign of wild life Jess had seen was a couple of buzzards circling a few miles back. The shoulders of highway 54 were beds of sand that showed evidence now and again where some un-knowing soul had driven off the pavement and become stuck. Then Jess's thoughts raced back to stories that he had read about the old cowboys of the 1800's and he wondered how the old timers had the grit to ride a horse through that dry, God-forsaken desert and how both man and horse must have suffered from the intense heat and dry conditions. They had to be tough men to endure such conditions. But there was no other way, they had to do it. The Lincoln Country wars had been fought near the area and this was 'Billy the Kid' country, thought Jess. No wonder that buck tooth Bill Bonney kid was so bad. Anybody that had to live and ride through hellish desert country like this on a mustang horse, well, it was enough to make a man bad.

As he sped along looking at the strange landscape, Jess came upon a sign that read 'El Paso 45 miles' and he knew that he was getting close to the beginning of search. Jess suddenly remembered the loaded twenty-five automatic and knew that he would have to throw it away before coming back across the border. He also knew that he would be doing some hard time in some Mexican jail if he were to be caught with the weapon. He had seen a documentary on 'Sixty Minutes' about the strict, Mexican laws pertaining to guns crossing the border. He had heard other stories about people being caught with weapons and Jess knew that there was no place in his life for spending time in some Mexican jail and the kind of treatment that might go with it. He eased the pistol down into the right boot holster that he had arranged to be sewn in by the local boot shop a couple of years back. The twenty-five automatic could mean the difference between living or dying and he remembered what he had promised Susan, 'I'll take care of myself.'

As Jess rolled through El Paso the interstate sign directed him to the port of entry and he drove directly for the border. There was no check necessary to enter Juarez, only a sign giving warning about carrying firearms across the border, which made the hair stand up on the back of his neck. He was illegal, that was for sure, but he didn't plan on having some thief slash his throat either. He had no time to be dead and Jess knew that he would never pull the gun unless it was life or death.

As he swept by the border patrol station, he hadn't traveled more than a quarter of a mile when he noticed in his rear view mirror a young Mexican who looked to be in his early twenties, peddling his bicycle as fast as he could after the truck. Jess slowed and young Mexican raced up along side and began to shout.

"*You want to go to market, No? I will show you what you want to know, pull over,*" he shouted in broken English.

Jess pulled the Ford over to the curb and the Mexican began telling him about his cousin's market.

"*I show you. Twenty peso! Twenty peso!*"

"Hold on, I am not interested in going to the market. I am looking for a race horse that has been stolen from me," said Jess.

"*I will show you many, many horses for you to see. Let me put my wheels in your truck and I will show you. Twenty peso!*" he pleaded.

Jess thought for a moment, and then agreed. It was for sure, he had to start somewhere and he might just get lucky and get a lead. The young Mexican smiled showing all of his teeth against his tan, leathery young face. Then he quickly put his bicycle in the back of the truck. He slid into the passenger's side of the cab and pointed the way. As they began to leave Juarez, Jess noticed the road sign indicating that he was on highway 45 and heading south. After they had ridden for about five miles, the young Mexican pointed to an area about a quarter of a mile off the road to the west.

"*Many horses to see . . . Racing horses,*" he said, still showing the teeth as he smiled.

He was absolutely correct. There must have been five hundred trucks, cars and horse trailers parked in every direction. Jess stopped the truck and pulled out five dollars and handed it to him. He smiled and quickly took the money. He bailed out of the truck and unloaded the bicycle.

"*I hope you find racehorse, amigo,*" he said, as he sped off back toward the north and the way they had come, in search of a new customer. Jess pulled the truck up to the area where the other vehicles were parked, opened the door, stepped out and pushed the electric door lock switch. He walked in the direction where all the noise was coming from.

As he broke through the crowd, he could see the broken down, partially white rails of a makeshift brush track. The track was undoubtedly a popular place on Sunday. There were at least a thousand Mexicans waving money in the air and shouting for some one to take their bet on their favorite horse. The track looked to be a quarter of a mile straight away with a short two foot high rail that probably needed to have been painted five or six years earlier. At the finish line there was a shack that stood on telephone pole stilts. It housed a public address system and the noisiest Mexican that he had ever heard.

Since Jess couldn't speak a word of Spanish, he suddenly felt helpless. His thoughts began to race and he wondered how he could communicate with anyone if Breathtaker was there. What would he do? How would he handle the Mexican thieves and take possession of his horse? Suddenly there was doubt in his mind, but he had grown up down in southeast Arkansas and had hunted all his earlier life. He had many times had to fight for what was right during his early years and he had learned the skill well from the school of hard knocks. He was also a woodsman and knew the value of quiet pursuit and stalking of game. His one-eighth Choctaw blood that he got from his great-grandmother had given him the natural ability to stalk quietly. Jess's father had taught him the ways of a woodsman and a hunter and he was a good marksman with a rifle or hand gun. He knew that he would possibly need every skill he had learned if the trail of the thieves were to lead into some unknown wilderness.

Jess walked on toward the starting gate area and knew instantly what the young guide meant when he said, "*Many horses to see.*" There were many to be raced, probably a hundred in all. They were all congregated behind the starting gates. There were bays, sorrels, palominos, blacks, grays, and any other imaginable color one could think of. Trainers were busy getting their horses ready to race. As Jess walked on searching for Breathtaker, two Mexicans were busy injecting drugs into a horse's neck in an effort to get advantage over their competition and that made Jess's blood boil. He walked on, skirting the area where the horses were concentrated, desperately looking for Breathtaker. A rather well-dressed Mexican in a three piece suit with a gold watch chain hanging from the vest pocket nodded his head at Jess and rolled out a line of Spanish. In an effort to answer, Jess nodded and tipped his hat. "No speak Spanish."

"*Oh, amigo, I am sorry. Did you come to enjoy a day of racing?*" he asked, in very good English.

"Well, not exactly, I'm looking for a gray racehorse that was stolen from me in Oklahoma."

"*He could be here. He is a good racing horse? No?*"

"Yes, he is a very good racing horse. I'm following up on a lead from the New Mexico State Police. They are positive that my horse crossed the border into Mexico a few weeks ago."

The man cast a sympathetic look at Jess. "*Amigo, you will not likely find your horse if you do not find him here today. This is a big country and many ways for thieves to go with a horse. But, you are in luck. I have a son that is a policia that has three weeks off from his work. If you will permit me, I will ask him to assist you with your search. He does not earn much money. He would like to work and perhaps assist you if you will pay him.*"

"I do not have a lot of money but I will pay him what I can if he will help me to look."

The man wiped the sweat from his brow with his handkerchief. *"We will look for your horse here first today then we will go to my casa and I will get him to talk to you. He speaks English and will be a great asset. My son is honest and knows the country well. He will help, I am sure."*

Suddenly Jess saw a gray horse and pointed him out to his new friend. The horse was the right size and had the same white sock on the right back foot. He had a red cooler draped over him. Jess's heart raced as they made their way through the horses. As they got near the horse, the Mexican friend rolled out a line of rather harsh-sounding Spanish and the little Mexican holding the horse instantly pulled the cooler off the horse. Jess suddenly felt a state of depression spread over his body and a sickness in his stomach. It wasn't him. The horse had saddle marks on his back from hard riding.

"Is this your horse amigo?"

"No, this is not him," Jess said as he turned and began looking at the other horses.

In an effort to console what he knew was an emotional letdown the man said, *"I am very sorry. I could see the look in your eyes and knew you believed it to be him. Do you need to look further?"*

"No, there's not much point. I've looked at all of them and he's just not here."

"Then we go to my casa and visit with my son."

"I apologize for not introducing myself to you. I'm Jess Steel form Sallisaw, Oklahoma."

"And I, amigo, am Tony Gonzales from Juarez, Chihuahua, Mexico," and he extended a firm hand shake.

Chapter 7

Jess followed the clean, neat, late model Buick the man was driving to a well-kept residential section of the city. He swung the Buick into the drive of a rather impressive Spanish style house with many arches decorating a court yard in front of the house. They pulled up and got out of the vehicles.

"Welcome to my casa," he said, very politely.

"Thank you, Tony, I'm very impressed. You have a beautiful home."

"Come, we will now talk to my son."

As the two men entered the impressive foyer, a pretty young Mexican girl who looked to be maybe twenty met them and took their hats.

"This is Teresa; she is my son's wife. My wife passed away five years back and they live here to help me. I have plenty of room in such a large casa and I am happy they are here. Where is that great husband of yours? He must talk with my friend."

The pretty girl smiled, *"I will get him, papa. He is taking a siesta."*

They sat down then Tony offered Jess some tequila.

"I thank you very much for offering. I might have only a little."

Tony poured the tequila. *"That is fine, amigo, I do not take much of the drink either."*

As the two men sat talking, a strong, well-built young man entered the room. He looked to be about six feet tall and in his early 30's. His tanned skin was a perfect setting for his well groomed mustache. He was wearing a pair of starched Levis and a bright-colored western shirt. Jess couldn't help but take notice of the handmade boots he wore. They were expensive boots. At least if bought in Oklahoma, they would be very expensive. He smiled and his pearly-white teeth exposed themselves through the jet black mustache.

"*Papa, who do we have here to visit?*"

"*My son, this is Señor Jess Steel from Oklahoma and this is my son, Emanuel. I am very proud of him. He is a good policía and a gentleman. My friend is here looking for a racehorse that was stolen from him in Oklahoma that crossed the border here a few days ago. He is willing to pay you if you will assist him in his search while you are not working.*"

"If you are interested, I will pay you what I can to help me. What would you charge me to help me search for the time you are off from work?

The young Mexican smiled. "*Amigo, I am not a rich man like my father, so I will be happy to work for you. I would sell to you all of my time, for say . . . one thousand peso or in American money that is roughly one hundred U.S. dollars, No?*"

Jess quickly said that would be satisfactory and they began to talk.

"*What kind of horse is your horse? Give me a full description. I have many friends across Mexico who know me well and will assist me in finding your horse,*" he said, as he looked Jess straight in the eye. Jess immediately gave him a full description of Breathtaker and as he talked, he squirmed a little. "Since you are a policeman, and you have agreed to help me in my search, what if I told you that I may be illegally carrying a weapon. What do you think about that?"

"*Amigo, there was no doubt in my mind that you were armed. You would be loco to search for your horse with out protection. It is good that you have a weapon. What kind of weapon do you have?*"

Jess reached into his right boot and pulled out the twenty-five automatic. The young Mexican began to laugh and Jess almost became offended.

Señor, I apologize for laughing so hard, but I must show you something."

He reached into his fancy, right boot and pulled out a twenty-five automatic exactly like the one Jess had shown him.

They both began to laugh. Suddenly the young policeman's disposition changed and a cold, serious expression came over his face. "*Señor, you are a man of good taste in back-up weapons and I think we will need such weapons if we catch up to the thieves that have stolen your horse. Will you use this gun if you have too?*"

Jess looked the young man straight in the eyes. "I will if it means living or dying."

"*We will make a good team, amigo, You have what I call, grit in your insides and that will help to keep us both alive. I, Señor, have used the gun many times to save my life or to apprehend a criminal. I will be ready to begin in the morning. First I have many calls to make to set up street informers so that they may look for us as well.*" The young policeman got up, shook Jess's hand, and walked toward the study located across the foyer from the living room.

"*Jess, you will stay here tonight. We have plenty of room and we will be happy you are in this casa. You cannot decline the invitation and that is final. Make yourself at home. I will tell Rosa we have guest. Rosa is our cook and she will prepare a special meal for you.*" Then Tony hurried toward the kitchen.

After the delicious dinner that consisted of beef enchiladas covered with green chili sauce, rice, re-fried beans and salad, they sat and talked for a while and then Jess excused himself and asked where he was to sleep. Tony quickly showed him to the guest room.

"Every thing is here, Señor. If you need anything additional, you need only ask."

"Thank you for your hospitality, Tony." said Jess, as he quietly closed the door.

Chapter 8

Jess Steel lay awake for an hour or more thinking about the conversation with Emanuel. He seemed to be a good man and sure seemed to be exactly what Tony had told him he would be. He was impressive to say the least, when he told of having to use the weapon many times. Somehow that gave Jess a secure feeling and seemed to solve one of his problems of great concern. Jess knew that he had told him that he would use the .25 if he had to. The thought of killing another man bothered him some, but Jess knew he would if he had to in order to protect himself. He also knew that Emanuel was concerned about his own safety if they became cornered and had to fight their way out of a scrape.

Jess's thoughts suddenly turned to Breathtaker, and he wondered if he had been fed that day. He didn't trust any lowlife that would steal a man's horse and he found himself becoming irritated at the thought. He pacified himself by thinking perhaps where Breathtaker was there was an abundance of grass. From total exhaustion and a day of searching for his horse, Jess rolled over and fell sound asleep.

Suddenly the peaceful sleep and the early morning stillness of the room were interrupted. Jess awoke to a knock on the door and realized that it was morning. Emanuel opened the door and announced that it was time to get up.

"Good morning, amigo. It is time for you and me to

get started with our search. While we were sleeping, the search was already launched and under way by my informants," said Emanuel as he closed the door and walked down the hallway of the immaculate home.

Jess quickly showered and dressed. As he walked down the hallway and entered the large dining room, Jess could see that a full breakfast had been prepared and was waiting. He was hungry but well rested from the long drive the previous day. He suddenly realized that he had not taken time to eat much since he left home and the dinner the night before was all that he had eaten in two days. Jess was hungry and the spicy aroma of food was all that was needed to excite a man's appetite. The two men quickly had breakfast and then Emanuel began to speak.

"Señor Steel, I received a call from an informant during the night. He believes that your horse is being held in a barn outside the city. We will go there and investigate the report. I know the man who is supposed to be holding the horse. He is heavily involved in drug trafficking into the United States and is believed to hide out in the mountains southwest of here. I also know that he and his men are killers and capable of killing at will. We will visit the area where the horse is being held and look closely at the situation before we proceed, after which, we will proceed with much caution. These criminals are not to be trusted. They will kill for the fun it."

Jess could see that his Mexican friend had grave concern about the task at hand. Jess suddenly thought about his Susan and remembered what he has promised her. He also knew that Emanuel wanted him to know exactly what they were up against. This could mean loss of either of their lives if they were not careful. Jess suddenly remembered what Emanuel had said about using the .25 automatic the evening before and he knew the Mexican meant business. He would not back up when the chips were down.

"Why would a drug trafficker be interested in

Breathtaker?"

Emanuel reached for the black western hat that lay in the chair beside him, placing it on his head. *"Amigo, the inside body cavity of horses is sometimes used to smuggle drugs across the border. The horse is operated on and plastic bags of cocaine are sewn up inside the body cavity of the horse. Once the horse is ready to ship, he is sent back across the border with the drugs. I do not know if this is the plan for this horse. Sometimes they purchase a horse, investing a lot of cash money and then sell the horse for whatever they can get in order to launder the drug money. I do not for sure know the situation. But it is now time to find out."*

They both got up from the table and started for the door. As they reached the door, Emanuel suddenly stopped and picked up a pair of .38 Smith & Wesson revolvers and two full boxes of cartridges he had placed on the table in the foyer the night before.

"Amigo, take this weapon and keep it hidden inside your shirt. Use this weapon as your primary means of defense. Only use your automatic boot weapon in an emergency situation. Both of these weapons are police property and there will be no problem associated with their use since they are assigned to me. With your permission, we will use your truck and trailer as a means of transportation but I will drive if you do not mind. I know exactly where we must go."

"Oh! Absolutely. It only makes sense, since. I don't have a clue as to where we are going."

The two men rode for ten or fifteen minutes south and entered a poverty-stricken area like none that Jess had ever experienced or seen before. There were people living in shacks that were nothing more than run down plywood shipping crates. There were a few chickens running loose, and now and again he could see a hog pen along the dirt street they traveled. Children were playing in the small makeshift yards, some with little or no clothing on their bodies. Many played in the street and would stop and sadly stare at the truck as Emanuel and Jess slowly rode by. Jess saw a man leading a donkey loaded with pieces of boards likely to be used for cooking. There were skinny dogs around nearly every shack. These were pets that needed food and care. They rode quietly for a while then Emanuel began to speak. *"Amigo, this area is something that you have not seen in your Oklahoma, no?"*

"No, I have not seen poverty to this extent and I don't understand why the Mexican government permits this kind of situation to exist or continue."

"It is simple, amigo. It is all about money. Without money there is no other choice. The children were born into the situation as were their parents. There is no other choice. This is why so many try desperately to enter the United States to work, only then to be turned back by authorities. Then they try to enter again and again".

"How much farther must we travel?"

"We have already passed the place where we are going to look for your horse, amigo. I am now only surveying the situation to get a feel for what we may face."

"I didn't see a barn back there anywhere,"

"It was there, you just did not recognize it as such. It was the old mission building sitting back off the street near the corner. We will circle and come back down the street behind it. I must know if it is occupied before we try to enter."

As they rode slowly by the back of the old mission, there was no sign of activity around the building. Emanuel pulled the truck off to the side of the street some hundred yards away from the mission and turned off the ignition. An old man with a walking stick hobbled down the road toward them and slowly approached the driver's side of the truck. Emanuel began to speak to him in Spanish. After they had talked for a while, the old man slowly walked on down the street tapping the ground with his walking stick. As Jess watched him leave, he noticed the walking stick appeared to be made from a cactus branch that he had removed the bark from.

"What did the old man say, Emanuel?"

"*He said it is true that a horse was unloaded into the old building four or five days ago and he is not sure if it is still there or not. He also said that a long black car comes to the building every day. He said that two men enter the building carrying buckets but he knows not why. Even though it does not appear that anyone is around, we will proceed with extreme caution. I will enter from the front and you will enter from the back of the building. I will give the call of a dove and that will be the signal to enter immediately with the weapon drawn.*" said Emanuel coolly.

Emanuel slowly made his way along side the old mission and disappeared into some brush that had grown up along the side of the building. Jess now knew exactly why Emanuel had such a serious look in his eyes the evening before. This was no picnic. This was downright spooky. This could be big trouble if someone were inside the building. He noticed that only small holes existed high up on the walls of the old mission where windows had once been. Jess knew that it would be rather dark inside and it would take a few seconds for the eyes to adjust to the darkness. He worked his way along the wall up to the back door entering the old building and crouched down awaiting the call that would inevitably come. Suddenly Jess heard the call of a dove and knew that it was time. Instantly he threw his weight against the door and twisted the hammered-steel door opener at the same time. As the door flew open Jess dove inside and scrambled off to the side out of the light and crouched still for a second letting his eyes adjust to the darkness of the building. He could see a little now and could make out the dim image of Emanuel at the other end of the building slowly making his way toward him with his weapon drawn. As Jess slowly made his way along a short, stucco wall to his left his heart pounded heavily and cold fear gripped his insides. Jess knew when he came to the end of the wall; there was no protection from that point on. As he approached the end of the wall that cold fear tingled up his back. He stopped. His heart was pounding and he knew this was the real thing. He suddenly swung around the end of the wall aiming the pistol with both hands ready to fire. As suddenly as Jess swung around the wall an old setting hen flew off of her nest at his feet, flapping her wings and squawking. Jess fell to the ground ready to fire at any movement, but there was no other movement. That was as scared as Jess Steel had ever been in his life. He managed to ease up on shaky legs and continue in a crouched position toward where he had last seen Emanuel. It was the longest walk of his life.

"It is vacant, Amigo; there is no one here now"

Even though Jess had reassurance from him that there was no one else in the building, he still eased along being extremely cautious.

"Amigo, the horse was here but he is now gone. I do not know for sure but he may have been moved during the night. Come and see."

As he approached, Emanuel looked at Jess. *"Your face is extremely white Amigo. What is wrong with you, are you a sick man?"*

"I'm sick all right . . . That ole hen came very damn near scaring me to death when she flew off of her nest,"

Emanuel was laughing. *"Amigo, I thought for a moment that you were going to shoot the poor chicken."*

Jess could see from the fresh droppings that the horse had been moved during the night. There were the tracks showing clearly the horse was wearing racing plates with toe grabs. He could also see a few grains of oats strewn near a make-shift horse trough and knew that Breathtaker had been fed. There was a water bucket partially filled with water that was with out doubt water the thieves had brought to Breathtaker. That gave Jess a good feeling and seemed to bring his blood pressure down a notch or two.

The two walked back toward the door where Jess had entered and stepped outside into the bright morning sun, which was already getting warm. As they neared the truck a young boy stepped from in front of the truck and began to speak. Jess listened intently as Emanuel discussed whatever it was the young boy was saying. They talked for a while and then Emanuel reached in his pocket and gave the boy a coin. As they climbed into the truck, Jess asked Emanuel what the conversation was about.

"The boy saw a truck leave the barn early this morning pulling a horse trailer. He said that a gray horse was riding in the trailer when it left."

"Did he say which way they went?"

"Yes, he said the truck went the direction we are now going."

As they continued slowly on down the dirt street, Emanuel stopped every so often and asked people if anyone had seen anything but was not having much success. They noticed a woman hanging clothes on a makeshift clothes line near the street. Emanuel pulled the truck up and shut off the engine. After some lengthy conversation, she pointed in the direction they were headed and swung her arm to the left. Jess then knew that she had given him some information.

"We are in luck, amigo, the woman said she watched the truck and trailer until it turned out onto the main road and then it headed south. That is a lead and that is all that we can hope for."

Emanuel sped up to the main road and turned south. *"Amigo, you should keep a sharp look-out for a red truck pulling a silver trailer. It could be anywhere and we must find it or get another lead from someone."*

They traveled for roughly fifty miles with no success in spotting the truck and trailer and then came upon a small cantina set off to the right side of the road. Jess could see a lone gas pump that stood along the side of the building. He noticed that there was very little sign of use. An old black-and-white spotted dog lay on the porch of the building as though waiting for a next meal to come. Some chickens strolled under the porch scratching in the dust for bugs and there was a milk cow tied to a picket stake at the rear of the building. Emanuel pulled the truck over and parked near the front of the building. *"Come, we will ask some questions and get something to drink."*

As they walked into the small dimly-lit room, a Mexican man sat near the end of the bar playing a rather large guitar, rendering a pleasant Spanish melody. Jess was fascinated with his expertise as he continued to play the guitar. Emanuel walked up to him and began to speak. Even though he had been addressed, he continued to play until the song ended. Then he leaned the guitar against the bar and slowly lifted the front of a rather large *sombrero*, exposing a smile. He then began to speak to Emanuel and it seemed that they knew each other well. The conversation lasted a long time and as they talked, a pretty young Mexican girl Jess guessed to be eighteen brought two glasses and a pitcher and set them on the bar where they were standing. She filled each glass and then looked at Jess and cast a teasing smile.

"Please have a cool drink Señor. It is made from the cacti that grow here," she said.

Jess picked up the glass and took a small drink of the liquid that she had poured. He had no clue as to what it was since it was not in a bottle but it was cool and he liked it.

"You like it, no?"
"Yes, I like it."
Jess noticed that it had a peculiar taste and a bite that made

the tongue tingle a little.

The girl smiled at Jess, *"My name is Falena."* She continued to expose her teeth through a beautiful tanned smile as she stood facing Jess across the bar. The white lace top that she was wearing hung low on one shoulder exposing smooth, dun cleavage.

Jess noticed that a double-barreled shotgun lay next to the music man at the end of the bar. Suddenly Jess thought of the words to the Marty Robbins song 'El Paso' and then he remembered what had happened to the man in the song. The man had been shot and had felt a bullet go deep in his chest over a *Falena.* Jess sure as hell wanted no part of the fireworks that double barrels could produce. The chicken had been plenty enough excitement for one morning.

Jess handed the other drink to Emanuel and sat down on a stool at the bar. The girl stood leaning against the bar with her elbows propped exposing more than necessary. She was almost in front of Jess and continued to look at him with her ever so teasing smile. Jess tried not to look at her as she flirted and talked. Jess drank slowly from the glass and feeling some discomfort he made limited conversation. Suddenly Emanuel's musician friend turned to Jess, *"It is ok for you to look at and talk to such a beautiful woman, Señor."*

Jess gulped the next swallow and almost choked himself. Oh hell, this is it. I'm a dead man now, he thought.

"She works for me, Amigo. She is a very good whore and does not cost much. The charge is only fifty peso."

"No, n, no, thanks . . . I . . . I . . . I'm a married man," stammered Jess, remembering what Susan had told him as he started out the back door.

Oh, yes Falena was exactly what Susan had called, a 'loose' woman. She was good-n-loose and a damn pretty woman to go with it. Jess Steel could smell death. He knew it could be right here in this *Cantina* if things didn't go right and it would surely be death at home if they did.

Falena continued to offer her pretty, teasing smile and push at her flowing, jet black hair that lay across her cinnamon shoulders. Jess suddenly became extremely uncomfortable. He got up slowly, tipped his hat to the girl, and eased his way over near the two men as they talked. Jess acted as though he could understand every word they were saying. Right then, he would do anything to avoid those dark, teasing eyes of Falena.

Chapter 9

As they got into the truck to drive away, Emanuel looked at Jess and laughed, *"Amigo, you are having quite an exciting day, no?"*

"All right, you've made your point so, it's been exciting. What the hell did the man say?"

"He is a man to be trusted. I know he can be trusted because I kept this man in the jail for thirty days and he knows that I will keep him there many more days if he lies to me. He said the two men pulling the horse stopped at his place early this morning and had breakfast. He listened to their conversation and learned they stole the horse from the drug dealer. It is their plan to race the horse in a race to be run this coming Sunday. He said they were talking about selling the horse after the race to a friend at Villa Ahumada some seventy miles south of here. He said they were very worried about getting caught with the horse and were going to hide out for a day or two. They had two other horses in the trailer so it may be possible they will leave the truck somewhere and go to a hideout and wait. They know the drug dealer would have them killed for stealing the horse."

"If we catch up with them and they are filling my horse full of drugs to run him, I will save this drug dealer some time," hissed Jess.

"Amigo, do not make statements that you are not sure that you can keep."

"I can keep them," snapped Jess, as his blood ran

hot at the thought.

"They have not changed directions, Amigo. They are now heading southwest and deep into Mexico toward the mountains. There are many places in this country where a horse can be hidden and match races are run. It will be, as you say, 'like looking for a needle in hay,' no?"

The two men rode on for almost an hour with hardly any conversation. Jess couldn't help thinking of how slim the chances were of ever finding Breathtaker. One thief steals the horse, then another thief steals him form the other thief. What kind of a place is this anyway? It would be a blessing if Breathtaker kicked the heads off of the two thieves, then maybe they could finally catch up to them. That is, if we were fast before some other thief stole him. Jess suddenly blurted out. "How did I get into this mess anyway?"

Emanuel took a serious look at Jess. "*Amigo, it is natural for you to become disgusted with the situation. I face this kind of situation every day of my life and it is not easy. You must take things in stride. It usually works out for the best and we may still find your horse.*"

Jess looked out the window toward the distant blue mountains to the west. "I guess I'm just not cut out to be a lawman."

Emanuel glanced over at Jess, through a wide grin. "*Yes, Amigo, I know that is right. But I also know that you handle yourself very well in most cases. Amigo, I also know that you are not cut out to be a . . . how shall I say . . . A ladies man. You were at a loss for speech while answering the man at the Cantina, no?*"

"Yes, old buddy, I confess, I was somewhat at a loss for speech... I guess."

They rode on for another half hour and entered a small village. Emanuel pulled the truck and trailer over to the side in front of another cantina. Jess suddenly thought about Falena and wondered how many of her type would be in this cantina. As they walked into the cantina there were two men sitting at a table near the back of the room drinking. A rather large Mexican with a handlebar mustache was behind the bar. Emanuel strolled over to the bar and ordered two drinks. As the bartender brought the drinks, Emanuel asked Jess to pay for their drinks with two five dollar bills. Jess pulled the bills out and laid them on the bar, "Damn, that seems kind of' high."

"*Amigo, just do as I say."*

Emanuel spoke to the bartender and the man reached out, pulled the two bills toward him, stuffed them in his pocket, and pointed to the two men setting at the table. Jess stayed at the bar while Emanuel walked over to the table and begin to talk to the two. They talked for a while and then Emanuel asked Jess to give them five dollars. Jess walked over and put the money on the table and returned to the bar. The conversation loosened up when one of the men began to speak rapidly. Jess now understood and knew that Emanuel was buying information. After they had finished talking, Emanuel came back to the bar and sat down.

"He is a friend of one of the men who have your horse. He said he talked to him this morning. One of them has a place down on the river to the south of here and they were going there with the horses. It is extremely rough country and we will need horses to go there. They have given me the name of a man who will provide what we need."

Emanuel motioned for Jess to follow as he began walking out of the cantina to go back to the truck. The main street going through the village was quiet. A dog lay on a boardwalk just outside of the stores and Jess could hear the rhythmic sound of a blacksmith's hammer shaping a horseshoe for a horse he was shoeing in front of the blacksmith shop. Two horses were tied to a rail along in front of the bank and a faded 1965 model Ford truck that had been lowered was parked along the curb near the horses. Emanuel drove on through the village and after a couple of miles he turned onto a dirt road leading up to a small, stucco house that sat about a half mile off of the road. As they drove up, Jess could see several horses in a corral that adjoined what looked to be a seven or eight stall barn. Off to the side of the house there was an old school bus that served as a chicken house. A dozen or so chickens were in a pen alongside the bus vigorously scratching the ground in search of insects but there was no sign of human activity anywhere around. Emanuel got out of the truck and walked up to the front door of the house and with his pocket knife he pecked on the porch floor four of five times. There was a rustle inside and then a short Mexican answered the door. He stood in the doorway and leaned against the door frame with one arm hidden behind the frame. Emanuel began to talk as the Mexican stepped out onto the porch. Jess saw the man point toward the horses as he stepped off of the porch. As the two men walked toward the corral, Jess got out of the truck and walked with them. The rancher showed them the horses and after some conversation Emanuel asked Jess to give the man a hundred dollars. The short Mexican tipped his hat at Jess and began to bow. *"Gracias, Señor,"* he said, as he walked toward the barn at a fast pace.

"Amigo, we have just bought two of his best horses as well as saddles. In addition he has two Winchester rifles along with ammunition that he has thrown into the deal."

Jess was looking at his new purchase. One of the horses was a heavy muscled tiger striped dun and the other was a dark bay with two back sock feet and a blaze face. The short man saddled both of the horses. Each of the saddles had saddle bags tied to the backs and they had been filled with oats for the horses. There were freshly-filled canteens hanging from each of the rather large saddle horns. Each saddle had a rifle sheath and in each sheath there was a Winchester rifle the man had taken from somewhere hidden in the barn. After loading the horses into the trailer, the Rancher handed Emanuel two full boxes of .30 caliber cartridges.

"Mucho Gracias, Señor," said Emanuel, as they waved and rode down the drive back toward the way they come.

Chapter 10

"It will be a difficult task to find which way they have taken the horses," said Emanuel.

Jess made no comment but knew that his skills at tracking would be helpful if there was any sign where the thieves had unloaded the horses. Emanuel drove through the village and headed south for a few miles. Suddenly Jess pointed off to their right toward the truck and trailer parked in an area of dense brush down near a small river that flowed from the distant mountains.

"There it is partner!" Jess pointed the truck and trailer out to Emanuel and then Emanuel swung the Ford into the dim road that led to the area and stopped a short distance from where the thieves had unloaded their horses. While Emanuel unloaded the horses, Jess skirted the area and examined it for tracks. Sure enough Jess found Breathtaker's tracks showing the 'toe grab' marks left by the aluminum racing plates. One of the other tracks indicated one of the horses was wearing a bar shoe on the right back foot, probably to correct a contracted hoof problem. Jess knew the racing plates and the bar shoe would be helpful in identifying the trail. The trail headed up river toward the mountains so the two men mounted and begun to follow the trail. It was an easy trail for Jess to follow in the soft soil of the river bottom so they rode at a canter for a long time before pulling up to let the horses catch their wind. They rode on for a while and suddenly Jess stopped, realizing there were no tracks. Jess pivoted the dun around and back tracked for maybe a hundred yards. He pulled up and began examining the ground closely. The ground was hard now for they were on an outcropping of gray shale that extended for about a hundred yards back away from the river. In the hard shale, down near the river, Jess made out a faint scrape left by the bar shoe and followed it toward the water. Sure enough the trail led straight into the river where they had crossed. Jess took the lead and pointed the tiger-stripe dun he was riding down the bank into the water. The river was not wide, maybe a hundred feet at the most, but it was deep enough for swimming the horses. As they pulled out on the far bank Jess could see the plain trail leading up the muddy bank. He knew that water would have been dripping from the wet horses when they climbed out of the river.

Jess looked at Emanuel. "They are two or three hours ahead of us!"

"How do you know that, Amigo?"

"No wet water marks on the ground. Water would have been dripping from their horses but it has already dried."

As they rode on away from the river the trail turned, continuing up river, and they followed. Now and again Jess could see scuff marks left by the racing plates. He smiled. He knew that Breathtaker was playing, kicking up his heels and frolicking as they led him on down the trail.

"Amigo, it is obvious that you are an expert at tracking. How far ahead do you believe them to be?" asked Emanuel.

They rode on for a few minutes and then Jess pulled the dun up, stepped down and began examining the tracks very carefully. Jess could see where a night crawler had crossed one of the tracks and other tracks revealed particles of dried dirt that had fallen back into the impression that the shoe had made. There was a weed that had been stepped on by one of the horses and it had already begun to straighten back up and a quail had dusted in one of the horses' tracks.

"They are four maybe five hours ahead of us now if I'm reading the signs right. That would put them ahead about ten or twelve miles if they keep their same pace. If they get into the mountains before we catch up to them we could lose them."

As they rode on quietly, Jess's mind wandered back to when he was a boy and the many times he had tracked deer through the big timber down in southeast Arkansas where he grew up. He remembered how his pa had taught him to track and how to search the ground, far ahead up a trail looking for leaves that had been moved or turned over or small pieces of broken brush or a small broken twig to identify a trail. His pa had told him many times that everything leaves a trail that can be followed if a man's senses are keen and he is willing to slowly study the movement of the pursued animal. He had also told him that a man on foot would leave the same kind of signs, just as an animal does. Of course, he always said that it must always be remembered, a man has the ability to try and cover his trail if need be.

Jess's great-grandfather had come to this country from England. He had grown up in the low, boggy, Fen country that lay partially covered with water. It was rough in those days and a boy had to fight for whatever he had and live the best way he could. He was orphaned and began working in the quarries when he was fourteen. He saved enough money to buy his way to America on a trading ship, and on his eighteenth birthday the ship set sail. After arriving in the new world, he lived along the coast for several years working the gold mines near Kings Mountain. Kings Mountain is located in what is now southern North Carolina. His grandfather had stayed in a small one-room rock cabin that had been built by a miner. The old miner who built the cabin had been killed by claim jumpers some time around 1790. Jess's great-grandfather lived there by himself, panning for gold during his early twenties. One time after eating breakfast he had spotted something lying on top of one of the pole joists that supported the roof of the cabin. He sat looking and studying the object for a few minutes but couldn't quite make it out. He could only see a small portion of the object, but it had a shimmer of gold about it. He quickly climbed up on top of the table to check it out and there, big as life, were four gold coins that showed mint marks from the nearby Bettchler mint where they had been cast. He continued to examine the coins and found they were twenty-dollar gold pieces, a great deal of money in those days. He sat back down studying the gold pieces and began to feel the urge to move, to travel. He had money now. After sitting and dreaming for a while, he packed up his few belongings and started west living off the land and fighting savages when necessary. Once the railroads began to move inland, he got a job working on the railroads. He was a tough square shouldered man who had known only hard work and the value of knowing how and when to fight. He survived in the New World and sometimes there was little, very little, to survive on. After he quit the railroad work he settled in the Indian Territory where he traded three horses for a beautiful Indian girl and she became his wife. They raised a family of eight children who grew up in the rugged mountains of what is now southeastern Oklahoma. They grew up hunting game for their food and blended in with the many Choctaws in the area. Even though her children were not full blood Indians, Jess's great-grandmother taught all them to speak the native language as well as the ways of her people. The oldest son was Jess's grandfather and he grew up hunting with the other Indian boys, learning their skills as well as those taught him by his father. When Jess's pa left home at the age of nineteen, he moved from Indian Territory to big timber country of South Arkansas but never forgot what he had learned. He knew that a foot wearing a moccasin left little sign and made traveling easy and silent. A soft sole would not snap a twig like a hard sole boot. He knew the value of being alert, watching the birds and knowing what their movements meant. He knew the difference in the scared flight and a casual flight of a bird or the call of caution form a bird or movement of an animal from fright. He had learned that slow movement around wild birds or animals would not excite them and they would become accustomed to and accept a human on those terms. He knew the value of good woods knowledge and its benefit. He had the ability to think and to plan and knew that good planning bred survival. In the old days, it was survival and the skills learned were necessary to stay alive in the wild country. That tough old Englishman who had migrated to the New World had passed this knowledge on to his children and his grandchildren and from Jess's pa on to him. Jess had not thought about his early training in a long time but now it was paying off. It was all coming back to him as he tried to catch up to the men who had stolen his horse.

    As they rode on up the trail, there was a rustle of water in the river and the cottonwoods whispered softly from the gentle wind above. Somewhere in the distance, a dove called to its mate and a coyote came out of its den in preparation for the hunt. Jess suddenly remembered that they had forgotten to get any kind of supplies and there was no telling how long they would be out there. No coffee… That was not good. Oh well, they would make the best of it and eat what they could find in the way of small game. He'd managed it many times before when he was a boy and he could do it again. Now all he wanted to do was find Breathtaker and take him home.

Chapter 11

It was getting on into the afternoon and shadows of the low-hanging timber cast long in the river bottom. Jess knew that darkness would come early since the sun would be going down behind the mountains. He suggested they begin looking for a place to camp for the night. Emanuel was not accustomed to hard riding as they had done for the large part of the day and readily agreed to stop and make camp.

As they rounded a turn in the narrow trail there was several large rocks that extended up higher than a man on horseback and behind them was a small green meadow with good grass for the horses down near the river. They pulled their horses up and dismounted.

"Amigo, I can hardly walk. I did not know that my legs were in such poor condition."

Jess laughed and discounted what the young policeman had said. It would be only a matter of hours until he was ready to ride once again. Jess knew that was the way it was when a man is as young as Emanuel, whether he was accustomed to riding or not. They pulled the saddle from the horses and led them down to the river to drink.

"We have traveled a long way Emanuel. I would never have believed those mountains were that far away when we started."

"This country will fool you, Amigo. It is big country"

After they had watered the horses and picketed

them on the fresh grass, Jess began pulling up pieces of bleached drift wood from the river. He would build only a small fire from the drift wood. The dry wood would not put off as much smoke as green, slow-burning wood. After he had enough wood piled up to last throughout the night, he took the .25 automatic out of his boot and walked back down the trail the way they had come and sat down on a log that lay beside the road. He hadn't sat their more than ten minutes when suddenly two rabbits hopped out into the trail and began nibbling on the tender, short vegetation. Jess eased the .25 up and took careful aim and squeezed the trigger. Again he squeezed and both shots brought down a rabbit. Jess knew the .25 would be hard for the thieves to hear since they were still likely two hours behind them, and too, the .25 did not make much noise. Jess field dressed the rabbits and brought them back to camp. Emanuel already had a small fire going so Jess cut a pieces of green willow about four feet long and two forked stakes to hold the willow up above the fire. The rabbits were quartered and threaded on the stick and allowed to roast slowly for a couple of hours. Both men were tired and hungry and the rabbit tasted good, even though they did not have the seasoning that would have been preferred. After they had finished the rabbit, they spread their saddle blankets down on the ground and lay down, placing their head in the saddle seats for pillows and talked for a while. Jess knew that the thieves had not spotted them yet because he and Emanuel had kept the cover of the river. And too, the thieves had probably just now reached the mountains.

"From here on, we need to proceed with caution, especially when we reach the mountains. We will be sitting ducks for ambush."

"That is true, Amigo, and these two men will not lose an opportunity to kill us if they have the chance. Once they determine that we are on their trail, they will quickly become desperate men and will do things they normally

would not consider."

They talked for a while and suddenly Jess heard Emanuel snoring. He had fallen asleep, so Jess closed his eyes letting his tired body relax. In only a few minutes he fell into a restful sleep.

Jess suddenly opened his eyes and he could see that the gray light of morning was upon them. He heard the hoot of an owl and then the gobble of a wild turkey somewhere up the river. He sat up and put his hat on. Putting on the hat was usually the first thing an Oklahoma cowboy did every morning. There was something about the hat going on first. If it didn't go on first nothing that he put on would feel right the rest of the day. Jess shook his boots to assure that a scorpion or snake hadn't found a warm home there during the night. He stood up, pulled them on, and stomped them in place. After he had re-kindled the fire with the toe of his boot he bumped Emanuel on the foot.

"Time to get up, ole partner, we've got thieves to catch."

There was no coffee and that was not good, at least as far as Jess was concerned. He liked that early morning coffee to wake him up and get him going.

Jess fed the horses oats from the saddle bags and after they had finished eating, the two men quietly saddled up. There was no coffee and neither of the two felt like much conversation. They needed coffee in the worst way and there was none to be had. They rode on up the trail at a canter for half an hour and then rounded a sharp turn in the trail. Suddenly Jess pulled up sharply and the dun skidded on his back heels to a calf-roping stop.

"This may be it, Emanuel. This may be an ambush."

Emanuel rode along side Jess, took a quick look, and then pointed. *"Look, amigo, through that small gap in the timber there. There's a cabin down near the river. This is the place that the informant told me about. We must proceed with much caution now, for they are killers."*

They dismounted and loose tied their horses to some low hanging brush off to the side of the trail and then stood for a moment planning and talking about what they should do next.

"I'll take the rear of the cabin, make my way down behind the river bank to the back of the house and then crawl up to back door through those tall weeds."

"That is a good plan. I will work around through the cottonwoods to the edge of the clearing over here. It looks as though I will be only a short distance from that point to the front porch. This is a time when you must shoot first. Amigo, these men are killers. We shall ask them questions later when they are lying very still," said Emanuel, with a cold, concerned look on his face.

As Jess worked his way along the bank he stopped now and again, removing his hat and then raising his head ever so slowly over the bank to look the situation over. There was no smoke coming from the cabin and it was quiet . . . too quiet . . . Then he noticed off to the west of the cabin, a small pole corral that had been built from debarked cottonwood poles tied together with rawhide. There were no horses. Jess thought about that for a minute and then decided they could have tied out away from the cabin on farther down the river. Jess noticed the back door to the cabin was slightly cracked but he could see no sign of movement inside. He worked his way a little farther along the bank and then cautiously eased his lanky, one-hundred-eighty-pounds over the top of the bank. He lay still for a moment listening for any slight sound that might come from the cabin. Nothing . . . As he lay listening, he remembered one time as a boy when he had crawled nearly a quarter of a mile to sneak up on a deer. He knew that he must make no sound, so he began to crawl carefully through the tall weeds. If he bumped the stalk of a tall weed it would have movement at the top that could be seen from the cabin. Working his way ever so slowly, Jess crawled to the edge of the weeds. Now he was only a short distance to the back door but had very little cover. He was within ten feet of the cabin now. He lay still listening but he knew he must move soon. Jess could feel his heart pounding in his chest and he was not sure if it was from the long crawl or from fear of a rifle that could come through that crack in the back door at any second. He eased his feet up under him then he was up on his knees. Suddenly he sprang up and lunged in a long leap up to the left side of the door and stood still, flat against the wall. He stood listening for movement inside for a minute . . . There was no sound . . . Nothing . . . There was total silence now. Using the barrel of the Winchester Jess suddenly pushed the door back hard and it slammed against the wall inside. Again there was no sound or movement that he could detect so Jess swung himself into the doorway, rifle ready from a hip position, but to his relief, the one-room cabin was empty. There was a partial pot of beans on the table and scattered food scraps lying about with a least a thousand flies swarming over the stale food. Four dirty plates had been left on the table and Jess felt of the coffee pot on the stove. It was cold. It looked as though there had been no one there for eight to ten hours. Suddenly the front door swung open and Emanuel stepped inside.

"*So, we were not lucky this time, Amigo.*"

"Oh yes, we are, there's at least a half a sack of coffee over there and a pot to boil it in."

They gathered up the pot, cups and coffee, and headed back to where they had left the horses.

"*Amigo, we shall have coffee in a few minutes. Then we will look over the situation to determine what we must do next.*"

Jess built a small fire and Emanuel brought up a pot of water from the river, pouring about a half hand full of coffee into the water. He then he set the pot on the fire to boil.

As they sat drinking the coffee, Jess could see through the cottonwoods that the river took a sharp turn around the base of the mountain to the north and he wondered if the thieves had stayed with the river or had ridden on into the mountains.

They drank their coffee and after finishing, tucked the remaining bit of coffee, the pot and two tin cups into Jess's bedroll and mounted up.

A dove called from somewhere out of the brush and the low clouds that had moved in before daybreak began to release a fine gray veil of mist and it looked as though they were in for a wet day. As they rode out a ways from the cabin, Jess found tracks left from four riders as well as Breathtaker's tracks. "They have picked up some company, Amigo. There are four riders now and that's double trouble, I'd say."

Emanuel surveyed the high rocks on the side of the mountain up ahead. There were a thousand places men could hide to take a shot at them.

"Amigo, we are in a dangerous situation. We must keep the cover of the river and use the timber as a shield until we reach the base of the mountains."

"Never fear, partner, we will do just that."

As they rode along slowly, Jess could see the trail had become rocky now and there was not much soil on the trail to expose tracks. He knew that he had to depend on other signs now in order to follow the trail. He took the lead riding slowly, looking closely far out ahead of them, finding a broken twig here or there or a scarred rock now and again to point the way. Straight ahead the mountain side towered upward and Jess could see a small opening to his left. As they rode on, the opening looked as though it could be leading into a canyon beyond. Jess looked back at Emanuel and motioned for him to follow. They worked their way slowly through a thick stand of aspen to the mouth of the canyon. The basaltic rock on the north of the narrow passage extended at least six hundred feet straight up and a small stream trickled through the mouth of the canyon, meandering its way down and finally spilling into the river that lay back behind them. It was a gloomy place to say the least and the dun didn't like it one bit. He tugged at the bit and shied. It was quiet, much too quiet to suit Jess. They stopped their horses near the mouth of the canyon and sat for a while listening and looking the rocks over carefully.

Jess whispered to Emanuel. "Amigo, look for unnatural objects, objects that shine or cast an unusual reflection. Look for unnatural color or the slightest movement of any kind. I've got a gut feeling they are here, Emanuel."

A faint breeze stirred out of the mouth of the canyon as though the breath of the devil himself had been released. It was quiet except for the leaves of the aspen trees whispering to the wind. They dismounted and then Jess caught the sudden flutter of a bird that flew from up in the rocks about a hundred yards away. Jess motioned to Emanuel to get down behind the rocks and stay there. Climbing ever so cautiously Jess eased his way up through the steep rocks, making his way ever so carefully so as not to disturb any lose rock. He eased up the steep incline keeping as much cover as he could between him and the place where he had seen the bird fly. Hunkering down, he eased the Winchester over a small bolder and rested the muzzle of the rifle across the top. He scanned the landscape inch by inch but he could detect no movement or sound up there anywhere. It was still now and the leaves above them quieted and the stillness gave way to his thoughts once again and he remembered the time when he was young and down near the mouth of the Arkansas River on a place called Big Island. He had been forced to climb a tree and had held up there, setting on a limb for several hours avoiding a wild razorback sow. He was only sixteen then and he had caught one of the old sow's piglets and when it began to squeal the mad sow showed up and the chase was on. The Island lay between the Arkansas and the White rivers that were connected to each other by way of a cut-off caused by overflowing high waters at some point in the distant past. The Island contained several thousand acres and was completely covered with virgin timber of various species. There were wild pecan, red oak, white oak, persimmon and several other types of hardwood that produced food in abundance for the wild game there. Along the slews, giant cypress trees grew, some with roots extending high above the ground, exposing wedge-shaped holes at the bottom of the trees with cavities inside the trees large enough for a man to live in. Some were as much a ten feet in diameter at the base. If a man wasn't a woodsman he could get seriously lost in that country because it all looked the same in every direction. It was a hunter's paradise, covered with deer aplenty, turkey and wild razorbacks and where there were wild hogs there was usually bear. Jess's mind suddenly cleared when he saw a slight movement at the base of a bolder about fifty yards away. He sat watching a small, dark object for a minute. It looked like a bird, but it stayed in the same position too long. It couldn't be a bird, he thought. It would have already moved. He continued to look at the object for maybe ten more minutes until the object moved a little. That time he picked it up. It was a man's foot, a black boot. It was definitely a boot extending out from behind the base of the bolder. He looked back down at Emanuel some thirty feet below and pointed toward the man and then pointed to his own boot. Jess took hold of the Winchester and slowly took aim. Careful and deliberate aim . . . He held the Winchester firm against his shoulder. He drew in a good breath and expelled about half of it and then held steady. He drew a fine bead, threw the sights, and squeezed the trigger. Fire belched from the rifle and the sound echoed through the canyon. A piece of the boot flew into the air and Jess knew the man would be operating on one leg now. He held his positioned aim, knowing the man had been hit and would possibly show himself. The man apparently didn't know exactly where the shot had come from and suddenly, dragging one leg, he lunged to take cover from an adjacent boulder. As the man passed between the boulders, Jess squeezed the trigger and the rifle belched once more. The thief did a flip backward and tumbled down the deep slope to the canyon floor, and he was dead. That's one . . . Now where are the other three? Jess sat for another thirty minutes very still looking at every slight movement of birds. Nothing . . . There was nothing up there and there was total silence now. An eagle soared high above the canyon and the leaves hung silent above . . . Then, Jess heard it . . . A sound . . . A click of metal. A cold chill ran down his back. The sound had come from his right and he knew that it was the hammer of a rifle being cocked. He spun, bringing the Winchester into hip firing position and then there was a blast straight in front of him and there was fire, fire in his face and a burning pain. Jess fell and hit the small ledge below him with a thud. Just as suddenly a blast erupted from Emanuel's rifle. Then not more than thirty feet to Jess's right a man rolled down out of the rocks off the slope and joined his friend in the silent, pits of hell.

    Jess laid still, blood trickling down the side of his face and his head pounding. He had been hit but he was not sure how badly. His head was wet with blood, his vision was blurred and his thoughts were all mixed up. He wanted to sleep, just a little sleep would help, but he knew that he couldn't. There were two others and they would likely show themselves now that he was down. Jess's mind cleared a little and he wondered what their next move would be. He had to think and plan, but he couldn't. He must think now . . . He must be alert . . . Their survival depended on it. He couldn't see nor hear Emanuel and wandered if there had been two shots. Was Emanuel dead? Just wait . . . He had to wait them out. He had to be ready for them when they came.

Chapter 12

   Jess looked at his watch. Two hours had passed since the shooting and his head was still hurting but his vision had cleared and he could at least see. The blood had dried on his face but still he didn't dare feel of his head for fear of starting the bleeding again. There was still no sound, nor could he hear or see any movement from Emanuel below. It was very quiet . . . There was total stillness except for the aspen leaves whispering softly to the breath of the wind that had picked up a little. His leg muscles were knotted and cramped but he dared not move for fear of the slightest sound that he might make. He eased his head ever so slowly over the shelf that he had fallen on and looked down. Emanuel was there . . . he was asleep . . . or was he dead? It was getting late now and darkness would be only a matter of minutes away in the shadows of the mountains. Suddenly the thought hit Jess that maybe there was no one else . . . Maybe the others had split off up the river or doubled back on the rocky trail coming up to the base of the mountain. They could have easily done that. Why hadn't he thought of that? But there was no way to be sure. Jess eased his cramping leg from under him ever so slowly and began to climb down the rock quietly. As he reached the bottom Emanuel opened his eyes and looked up at him.

   "I thought you were dead, Amigo. I was sure of it when I saw you fall over. Here, let me have a look."

   Emanuel removed Jess's hat and parted the hair

where the blood had dried.

"Oh . . . *but you will live to fight again, Amigo. The bullet only grazed your head, cutting the skin.*"

"Stay here, Emanuel, I am going to ease my way up into the canyon and take a look before it gets dark."

Jess eased along making his way slowly through the thick aspens, stopping and looking in every direction every four or five steps. He would remain in the same position for a little while and then he would move forward very slowly, not taking more than four steps . . . Stalking . . . ever so slowly . . . He looked ahead into the canyon and could see that it covered an area of about ten acres. The canyon floor was covered with rich grass, dotted with yellow wild flowers mixed with stands of purple sage. It was beautiful country, thought Jess. The canyon narrowed about quarter of a mile ahead, forming a box canyon. Suddenly through the thick brush to his right below the canyon wall, he saw movement . . . It was movement all right. He stood perfectly still, looking out of the corner of his eye toward where he saw the movement. He had learned a long time ago that a man could catch movement better out to the side of the eye, not looking directly at an object. Then suddenly it moved again and he made it out. He could barely see the image of a horse through the brush. It was a bay and then he saw a little further another horse, a sorrel, both tied near the canyon wall. Jess straightened up feeling relief. So that's it . . . He swore quietly. Hell yes . . . There where were only two. Why hadn't I thought about that before? He walked on out to where the horses were tied, unsaddled them and set them free into the canyon. He walked back to where Emanuel was waiting and smiled. "Let's get out butts out of here. The other two have doubled back."

They mounted and rode out away from the base of the mountain and it was not nearly so dark after getting out of the shadow of the mountains. Jess scanned the trail, looking for anything that would indicate the others had turned off the trail but saw nothing. Suddenly he drew up and pointed to a thorny mesquite bush off to his right a dozen feet away then rode over to it. "That's the kind of thing I've been looking for, Emanuel. See that little piece of blue thread hanging on that thorn? It's about a half inch long and it's a thread from a saddle blanket and there, see that broken twig? Hell, those suckers left a trail a blind man could follow. They've turned off here and headed south," he said.

Jess followed the faint trail that led out of the river bottom into the edge of the desert and then pulled up.

"Well, they did just what I thought they had done. See here, here's Breathtaker's track and there's a track left from the bar shoe on the other horse." They rode for a few minutes and the trail began to turn back to the east and it was obvious the men were in a hurry and riding at a fast canter. Their trail continued to head east for a while and then it turned back toward the river.

Jess pulled up his horse and swore quietly.

"What is wrong, Amigo?"

"Looks like we've been foxed my friend. They must have spotted us late yesterday or they were close enough to hear the .25 when I shot the rabbits. That's when they saddled up and circled around us. The thieves rode in the dark last night and headed back down river. Their tracks are several hours old and that tells me they were riding while we were sleeping. Pretty clever, I'd say. They left the other two men to kill us from ambush."

"Do not worry, Amigo. We will catch them and for this long ride and the soreness of my rear end, we shall make them pay dearly. Oh, yes, Amigo . . . they will pay."

They continued following the trail at a gallop until it tied back into the trail at the river where they had ridden in.

"I don't see any need to push on. It's about dark so

we may as well make camp and rest for the night and get an early start in the morning," said Jess.

They dismounted and unsaddled the horses. Emanuel picketed the horses and Jess went to the river and washed the dried blood form his face and head. The cold water felt good on his face, but the water burned the wound as he tried to clean the dried blood out of his hair. After he finished, he gathered an arm load of the drift wood and brought it back to the camp, built a fire and made a pot of coffee. There was still a feeding of oats in the saddle bags, so Emanuel carried the oats out and poured them into two piles for the horses.

They spread the saddle blankets out and there was very little talk between them. They were tired and fell asleep quickly. Jess dreamed crazy dreams of men shooting at him and of him running into a big fire to avoid them. Suddenly Jess, opened his eyes and from the dim reflection of the burning coals he could barely see his watch and it was time to get moving. It was five- thirty. He re-kindled the fire, filled the coffee pot out of his canteen and set the pot on the fire. After he had the coffee on, he walked out to the horses and led them to the river to drink. They were thirsty and drank in long gulps from the cold river water. After they had finished drinking Jess led them back to the fire and began saddling them. Emanuel was up by this time and sat silent, drinking coffee. Jess poured himself some coffee and stood looking into the fire. Emanuel remained seated where he was and Jess knew that he was dreading to climb back into the saddle.

"Amigo, you are a lucky man to be alive. If the bullet had been one quarter- inch lower it would have split your skull and you would be very dead."

"I thought I was a goner anyway. I can still see that fire in my face and the burning hot feel of the lead. I knew that I had been shot but I couldn't think clearly enough to determine how bad or where I had been hit. At least my head don't hurt so badly this morning. It's just sore."

They mounted and rode at a fast canter most of the way, only stopping periodically to let the horses catch their wind. At mid-morning they crossed the river and finally made it back to where the trucks and trailers had been parked. Sure enough the thieves' truck and trailer were gone, leaving only Jess's truck with a flat tire on the right front that exposed a knife hole in the side of the tire.

I don't know how we lucked out, but the other tires have not been cut," said Jess as he came around from circling the truck.

The angry young lawman looked at Jess and frowned. *"Amigo, that was just to let us know they had out foxed us if we made it back from the ambush. That is all right for them to make such a stupid gesture. I will have my revenge in time."*

They changed the tire, putting on the spare and loaded the horses into the trailer. Emanuel headed out toward the main road. As they came near the main road, Jess asked Emanuel to stop. Emanuel pulled up and Jess walked up ahead and checked the tire marks and quickly returned to the truck.

"They turned south, Emanuel. Where does this road go?"

"I am not sure where the road ends but there is a village about fifty miles ahead and we shall go there and ask questions. They will not likely be in a big hurry. They will believe that we are in the mountains very dead."

The two men were quiet as they rode on south. After they had traveled for a good hour, they entered the village. It was getting late in the afternoon now and the streets were alive with activity.

"What is going on here? Why so many people?"

"Amigo it appears that a fiesta is underway," said Emanuel.

There were donkey-drawn carts parked along the

side of the street. The carts were decorated with brightly colored paper. The spokes in the wheels were laced with aqua and pink paper woven neatly. The donkeys were decorated with ribbons and now and again one would have a large bow tied in its tail. Even the dogs on the street were decorated. A Mexican band was playing and many beautiful Señoritas wearing brightly colored skirts and sparse white tops were dancing to the sound of the gala music that filled the street. The aroma of Mexican food and roasting corn filled the air. There was a greased-pig-catching contest going on. The participating youngsters were greasy all over. Jess couldn't tell who had the most grease on them the kids or the pig. Emanuel pulled the rig up in front of a cantina and turned off the engine.

"I take it that it's question time again," said Jess.

Emanuel looked over at Jess, *"No, it is coffee time again, Amigo. It is long past time for good coffee that has not been boiled."*

After they finished their second cup they paid the girl who had waited on them and strolled outside.

Far down the street near the end, there was a large crowd of people gathered waving money in the air.

"What are they betting on, Emanuel?"

"Amigo, it appears that we are in luck. If we can get beyond the crowd of people, I'm sure that we will find a horse race about to begin."

"Does a horse race normally attract so much attention and create such a festivity?"

"Si, Amigo, if it is a special race and this one appears to be such a race. Come, we will see what is going on here with the horses."

Jess started walking in the direction of the crowd and as he did he felt for the thirty-eight to assure himself that it was still there and ready.

As they made their way through the crowded street,

they broke through the crowd and suddenly Jess's heart jumped into his throat. There he was . . . Breathtaker was standing calmly awaiting his time to race. Jess felt the blood rush to his face and Emanuel knew instantly that they had found the horse.

"It is him . . . is it not?"

Jess was so excited until he could hardly answer him.

"That's him all right. What do we do now," Jess asked, in a whisper.

Emanuel whispered. *"You must stay here out of the line of sight when I approach the thieves. It would not be safe for you, an Americano, to be seen by the thieves and it would make their apprehension almost impossible for they will run. It is my feeling that we should wait until the horses have run the race to make the move. There is much money bet on the horses and to stop the race would cause much excitement and perhaps death to many."*

Jess's face showed deep concern. "What if Breathtaker injures himself or breaks a leg on the rough terrain? He has never run on hard ground,"

Emanuel's eyes were cold. *"Amigo, I know you have grave concern for your horse, but this is a chance we must take. It is too dangerous to do otherwise."*

Suddenly they saw two men approach the young Mexican holding Breathtaker.

"That will be the two thieves described to me by the man at the Cantina. We will change our plans now that we know their presence. I know one of the men. He is only a common thief and not considered to be brave."

Emanuel suddenly spoke to a man standing near by who was wearing a large *sombrero*. The man quickly pulled off the hat and handed it to Emanuel.

"Give him two dollars for the hat and put it on quickly now. The race is about to begin. We will work our way around and get near the two men and wait for the race to end. When the excitement is underway at the end, I will

suddenly take the larger man with the red shirt and you apprehend and secure the short man wearing the western hat. Here are some handcuffs for you to use. You will be on your own, Amigo. You must do things right. Do not make the mistake and not search him after you have him on the ground and in handcuffs. He may be armed. Now we get in place and see what we are made from."

The thought of being able to slug one of the thieves somehow seemed exciting or maybe the thought of Breathtaker about to run off and leave someone's cow horse was the reason, but Jess actually laughed out loud as they made their way up near the two thieves who stood watching.

The crowd suddenly quieted and a Mexican standing in the back of a donkey cart held a pistol high ready to fire for the start of the race. A small Mexican was riding Breathtaker. Breathtaker stood quietly, seeming to know that he was about to run. The young Mexican upon his back suddenly slapped him on the neck and Breathtaker shied to the left quickly not understanding the fierce slap on his neck. The other horse was a big bay horse with powerful haunches and a rather common head that was unmistakably someone's cow horse. Suddenly the gun fired and the Mexicans screamed at the horses. In one lunge Breathtaker left the other horse two lengths behind and was running easily, leaving his competition with each powerful stride. It was no match and the challenging rider pulled up his horse in disgust. There was a roar from the crowd and instantly Mexicans were paying the two men with fistfuls of *Pesos.* Emanuel whispered to Jess.

"*Amigo, you must wait until I give the signal and we shall get a bonus and apprehend the thieves as well."*

They waited for what seemed to be five minutes for the men to collect their money then suddenly Emanuel whispered to Jess. *"Now Amigo! Now!"*

Jess sprang toward the smaller man, grabbing him by the arm and spinning him around, and delivering a hard right to the left side of the man's chin that staggered him. The thief responded, quickly punching viciously as Jess weaved, bobbed and ducked causing the thief to miss his mark. The Mexican punched again with a left then a right, both punches deflected by Jess's arm. Jess countered with a left that missed the mark and then he threw a driving right that landed solidly on the bridge of the thief's nose. Jess heard the nose break and a gush of blood spouted from the man's face. Suddenly the thief hissed profanity and pulled a knife from inside his shirt. He began circling around to Jess's left side. The thief held the knife low with the blade's cutting edge in an upward position. It was obvious to Jess that the thief knew how to knife fight and as for him, he knew nothing of how to defend against a knife. Jess watched the ugly knife and realized that it seemed to have a hypnotic effect on him. Jess kept his eyes trained on the blade and knew that he must avoid the knife by any means. Suddenly the thief slashed at his throat, barely missing. Jess felt the wind from the blade and the hum of the weapon's movement as it stung his neck again. Jess knew then that he must kill him with the pistol or get a death hold on him quickly. The Mexican slashed at Jess's belly, barely missing, and suddenly Jess countered with a hard left to the side of the head. The thief again circled to the left hissing words that Jess could not understand. The short man lunged at Jess just missing and slashing the sleeve of his shirt. Jess was helpless unless he just drew iron and outright killed the man. The Mexican lunged at Jess again just missing his face with the knife. Jess saw his opportunity and took advantage of it. He slammed a hard right to the man's stomach and the thief folded down from the lack of air. Jess slammed his right knee upward into the man's face and he felt teeth shatter against his leg. The Mexican's hat flew off and the knife went sailing through the air and Jess knew the fight was over. The man's short legs buckled and the thief fell face down and then rolled over onto his back. By the time he hit the ground Jess sprang on top of him, placing his knee on the Mexican's head. Jess couldn't see how many but there were several teeth on the ground beside his head. Blood was flowing freely from the man's face as Jess kept him pinned securely. Keeping his foot on the man's head, Jess reached out and picked up the knife and tossed it further to the side. He secured the handcuffs tightly around the wrists and then shook him down for additional weapons. Jess pulled a cheap handgun from the thief's right back pocket and tossed it to the side. He lifted him to his feet and turned toward the scuffle going on between Emanuel and the other man. Emanuel had his man down but the man was a big, stout Mexican and Emanuel was having a hard time getting the handcuffs on him. Suddenly Emanuel reached in his pocket and pulled out the thirty-eight. Jess knew that Emanuel was going to kill the man. Then Emanuel suddenly swung the flat side of the pistol hard against the man's head, knocking him as cold as a ripe persimmon on a frosty December morning. Emanuel looked up at Jess and smiled through his jet black mustache as he secured the handcuffs. *"That was for making me ride the horse so long."*

Emanuel quickly jerked the leather pouch full of money loose that the thief had tied to his waist.

"Oh, yes, amigo, It is fun to catch a thief and get a bonus at the same time, no?"

Jess looked around to see about the money that had scattered when the other man hit the ground. There was no money left anywhere nor was there a Mexican in sight. Emanuel began to laugh.

"You must get the money quickly down here, very quickly, or it will disappear."

Jess smiled. "So what? I got my horse old buddy, I got my horse"

Jess pushed the short thief over to where Emanuel had his man pinned up against the wall and Emanuel took an additional pair of handcuffs and hooked the two men together.

Jess didn't care how much Emanuel laughed, he didn't come after money anyway. He came after Breathtaker and he was finally going to get his hands on him. The rider had long since disappeared and Breathtaker was grazing on tender shoots of grass some fifty yards away as though nothing had happened. As Jess walked up to him, Breathtaker raised his head and placed his nose into Jess's chest and nickered softly just as he had done so many times before back home. Jess reached out and rubbed Breathtaker's soft velvety neck for a moment and then with his right hand he reached into his pocket, pulled out a cube of sugar that he had been carrying and gave it to Breathtaker. Jess had taken it out of a sugar container at a truck stop somewhere in the Texas panhandle four days earlier just for that occasion. "Now we can go home, boy," said Jess.

Chapter 13

Jess Steel led Breathtaker back toward where he had left Emanuel holding the two thieves. Emanuel was having an extensive conversation with them as Jess walked up. Emanuel drew back his fist and pushed it hard against the face of the short man as he continued to talk to him through clinched teeth. He knew Emanuel was mad and he meant business. He also knew that he was either trying to get some information from the sullen man or punishing him for the ride that he had had to take. Suddenly the short man began to speak nervously. He rattled on for what seemed five minutes and Emanuel spun him around and slammed him hard against the wall of the nearby building.

"Emanuel, ask them if there is a livery stable where we can bed Breathtaker down?"

Emanuel began to address the short, sullen Mexican once again. The short man did not answer and Emanuel again slapped him across the face and jammed him hard against the wall. Suddenly, the thief began to point and talk at the same time.

"Si, Amigo, there is a livery stable down the street and a small hotel as well," said Emanuel.

"Oh no . . . no hotel for me, this time I will sleep in the livery stable with Breathtaker," said Jess.

Emanuel looked at Jess and smiled, *"Then I too will stay in the livery stable. You may need help during the night with the horse."*

Jess knew that Emanuel didn't believe for one

minute that he could possibly need help with the horses. He was afraid that someone might try robbing Jess to take Breathtaker during the night. That was it in a nut shell.

"Amigo, I must take these two hombres' to the local calaboose and lock them up. Wait for me here, I will return in a short amount of time. We will then go to the livery stable and attend to the horses."

Emanuel pushed the two bloody thieves in the back with his foot, heading them toward the jail. They both were sullen and rolled out a harsh line of Spanish.

While Jess waited for Emanuel to finish the business of locking the two up, he unsaddled Breathtaker and rubbed his back down with the small saddle blanket. Breathtaker stood quietly as Jess stroked his back and talked to him. He was sure happy to be getting the attention. The colt seemed to know that Jess was glad to see him. Breathtaker nibbled lightly at the back of Jess's shirt as he continued to rub him down with the blanket. Yes, sir, he was one fine colt, thought Jess. Jess ran his hand down Breathtaker's legs and then picked up each of his feet and checked them closely but found no damage. Jess rubbed down his front legs for a while and at the same time checked them for tendon damage. He seemed to be just fine and none the worse for wear. Breathtaker was lucky with all the hauling and the rocky trails he'd been on for the past few days, and the hard ground that he had been forced to run on. Jess noticed all of the aluminum racing plates were still in good shape and tightly nailed.

Jess looked at his watch. It had been a good forty-five minutes since Emanuel left with the two men and Jess became uneasy and wondered if his friend had run into more trouble. Suddenly Emanuel came around the corner of the building with a big smile on his face and carrying a brown paper bag.

"Amigo, now we care for the horse, then we will

eat. I found tamales with much chile peppers. They will be good ones."

Jess knew then that he was in for a bad night. The tamales would be hot as fire but as hungry as he was, he would eat them and like the heat. It beat rabbit with no salt that was for sure.

Emanuel and Jess led Breathtaker down the dirty, paper-littered street toward the livery stable. Several men standing in front of a cantina spat out lines of Spanish and one of them pointed toward Breathtaker as they passed by. As they entered the wide door opening leading into the livery stable Jess could see that it had two large doors made from rough-sawn lumber that led to the outside in the back. An old man met them and began to speak. Emanuel talked to him for a minute then the old man pointed to several places inside the barn. He walked to a small stack of hay that was near the entrance and pulled out a bale of hay. He hobbled over to a small room near the hay and poured a gallon bucket full of grain.

"The hay and grain will cost five pesos. The stall for the horse will be five pesos and space for us will be an additional five pesos as well. That is a total of fifteen pesos that you must pay in advance."

Jess pulled out five one dollar bills and gave them to the old man. "He gets a bonus."

The old man smiled and began to bow. *"Gracias, gracias, Señor, mucho gracias,"* he said, as he tucked the money deep into his front pocket. He quickly took the bridle reins out of Jess's hand and led Breathtaker to a stall near the center of the stable. The old man was excited about the five dollars and it was evident that he certainly meant to accommodate in every way that he could. After closing the stall door, he again began to speak in Spanish to Emanuel and they talked for a while. Emanuel pointed toward the back door of the building and then to the hay stacked near the front. The old man lifted his sombrero from his head and said good-by. That was probably the only word of Spanish that Jess understood.

After the old man had left the building, Emanuel pulled down two more bales of hay from the stack to be used to sit on. He opened the sack, took out two bundles of tamales and spread them out onto the paper sack.

"Amigo, it is now time to eat."

Jess carried the bucket of grain to Breathtaker's stall and gave him half of it and saved the balance for his breakfast. He noticed that the man had already put water in the bucket hanging on the wall. Jess hurried to the bale of hay and sat down. The tamales that Emanuel had opened were large ones bundled and tied with six in each bundle. They looked and smelled delicious. Jess unrolled one of the tamales from the corn husk it was wrapped in and took a large bite. It was delicious. He quickly took a second and bite then . . . fire hit powder. It was full of hot chili peppers that made Jess's eyes water and left a burning sensation all the way around his mouth. Emanuel began to laugh as he handed Jess a cup full of water from the sack.

"It is hot, Amigo?"

Jess managed to get one word out.

"Si"...

After they had eaten and talked for a while, darkness fell upon the village. There was no light in the barn other than a lantern hanging by the front door that Emanuel had lit. The lantern cast amber light inside the barn and Jess could scarcely make out the image of Breathtaker as he pulled large mouthfuls of hay from the rack and chewed each bite slowly. Jess and Emanuel lay back on a stack of loose hay and fell sound asleep. Jess didn't know how long he had slept when suddenly he was awakened by a noise and movement at the front door to the barn. Jess slid his hand slowly down and took hold of the thirty-eight and then lay still for a second listening for footsteps. It was extremely quiet now and there was no movement. He lay still for what seemed five minutes. Suddenly there were flashes of fire and the rapid sound of gunfire erupting. Several shots rang out shattering the night air. Jess could see the fire flash from two weapons and knew that Emanuel was firing his weapon as well. Someone opened the front door and then he heard running. Jess was so startled by being awakened out of a deep sleep that quickly and with excitement from the gunfire that it made him shake inside. Jess called out to Emanuel but there was no answer. As he lay quietly, Jess wondered if the runner was Emanuel. Suddenly the front door opened and a strong flashlight beam hit Jess directly in the eyes. The intruder lashed out with a harsh line of Spanish of which Jess did not understand one word. The light scanned the area near the front door and then Jess saw in the beam of the light that Emanuel lay motionless on the hard dirt floor. The intruder suddenly asked, *"Are you Americano?"*

"Yes . . . I. . . . I'm Americana. My name is Jess Steel and that other man is my friend and he, he's been shot by someone who entered the barn."

The stranger kneeled down and rolled Emanuel over.

"Oh, yes, I know him, Señor, he is the policia who brought the two thieves to my calaboose this afternoon. I am very sorry, but your friend, he is very dead, amigo," he said.

Jess was still trying to come to some realization as to what exactly had happened.

"Who would want to kill this man? We were only sleeping here," said Jess.

"My Americano friend, you are now south of the border. Your friend was a policia and there are many that would kill him just for the chance. He continued, "Do you know this man's family?" asked the lawman.

"Yes, he is the son of Tony Gonzalez in Juarez. His

name is Emanuel."

"I know his name is Emanuel. He introduced himself to me this afternoon but did not tell me his last name. He only gave me his first name and a telephone number where he could be reached if I needed to reach him in the future."

"The number he gave you is probably his father's number," said Jess.

"Come with me, we will call the number and notify the family of this man's death," said the fat Mexican policeman, as he turned and walked outside. Jess quickly took the truck keys out of Emanuel's pocket and noticed that the money pouch containing the race winnings was not there.

Chapter 14

After the policeman had called Tony and notified him of his son's death, Jess felt choked up inside and sick to his stomach. He felt nothing but the deepest of sympathy for Tony and his family. Listening to the conversation, Jess knew that Tony or someone was on the way down to get his dead friend's body. Jess went back across the street to the livery stable and fed Breathtaker and the other horses the balance of the grain left from the night before. Then he filled the water buckets. Jess sat down on a bale of hay and thought about what they had been through the past few days and knew that Emanuel's killer needed to be caught and punished for such a brutal act. He also knew that it was very unlikely that much effort would be extended toward finding the killer. After he had sat for an hour he wandered back across the street to the jail. As he opened the door and stepped inside, he could hear a heated discussion between the lawman and an old Mexican rancher. The lawman looked at Jess as he came in.

"Señor, this is the day for trouble in this village. This man says that he too lost one of his best horses to a thief such as the one that stole your horse."

"Do you believe that the man who killed my friend stole his horse?"

"Oh no, Señor, the man that killed your friend was said to have fled in a truck. The man that stole his horse headed out into the desert with him and only a fool and common thief would do such a thing. A killer would never

be such a fool as to try and go there. The closest water hole in the desert is a day maybe two days ride to the northwest."

The Mexican rancher shook his head and began waving his hands in disgust. It was apparent that he was not going to get much cooperation form the law so he stomped out of the jail in a state of frustration. Jess followed him outside and tried to ask him where he lived. The rancher did not speak any English so Jess began making hand motions in an effort to communicate and get him to show him where he lived. After a few minutes of hand signals, a young Mexican girl came out of a store and saw the problem that Jess was having communicating.

"May I help?" she asked, in very good English.

"Oh yes. You sure can. I would like this man to show me where he lives and the tracks of the horse that was stolen from his place this morning."

The girl began talking to the rancher and discussed the matter for a fair amount of time.

"Señor, it is true that the trail of the thief leads into the desert but he says that he is too old to try and catch the thief."

"Ask him if I can leave one of my horses with him and I will attempt to capture the man and bring back his horse," said Jess.

She talked to the rancher for a little while and Jess knew that it was agreeable because he watched his reaction and heard him say: *"Si."*

Jess asked the girl to have the man wait for him at the truck. "Also tell him that I must get some food to take with me if I am to try and catch the thief."

The girl told the old man what he had said and Jess asked her if she would go with him into the store to help translate for him so that he could make his purchases quickly. She smiled and promptly agreed to help. They entered the store that she had just come out of and Jess immediately began picking up the items that he needed. He bought a two day supply of canned meat, salt pork and beans, two canteens for water and a good supply of beef jerky, salt, and pepper. Then he spotted a coil of half inch cotton rope. He pulled off about thirty feet of the rope and cut it with his pocket knife. He paid for his goods and they left the store. Jess thanked the girl for her help and gave her a two-dollar tip. She said good bye and happily walked on down the street. Jess and the aging rancher went down the street to the livery stable. He went into the barn and led Breathtaker and the other two horses out of the barn and loaded them into the trailer. Jess slipped into the seat and cranked the engine. The old rancher immediately began to give hand signals as to the route to take. Jess wondered if he was making a big mistake, but he had a hunch the fat lawman was wrong about the killer leaving in a truck. It was a chance he felt that he must take. After all, Emanuel had worked extremely hard trying to help him find his horse. Helping to find the man who killed his friend who had helped him so much would be the least he could do.

    They hadn't gone more than a couple of miles when the rancher pointed to a small, stucco ranch house and rather large barn that sat about a quarter of a mile off the road. A lightly used dirt road lead up to the house and Jess noticed that there were several good looking horses in the pole corral as they drove up. Jess stopped the truck and began to unload Breathtaker, the dun, and the bay. The Mexican rancher trotted to the barn leading the dun. Jess held Breathtaker while the old man saddled the big, stout, bay gelding that Emanuel had been riding. Jess noticed the bay looked like he could run some and led him out and started to mount, but then thought about having the supplies. He opened up his bedroll and rolled the supplies in the bedroll while the old man filled the canteens with water. After everything had been secured on the back of the saddle, Jess stepped in the stirrup and mounted up. Then the man showed him the horse tracks leading out into the desert. Jess tipped his hat to the man, dallied Breathtaker's lead rope to the saddle horn and headed out. The trail was easy to follow in the sand so Jess rode at a canter for a while before letting the horses blow a little. Breathtaker was fresh and as they rode he bucked and kicked up his heals. Jess knew Breathtaker would stop playing after a few miles so he just let him play.

It was now 11:00 a.m. and Jess knew if his hunch was right the trail the thief was taking would put him in the distant mountains to the northwest some time tomorrow afternoon. Jess also knew that the distant mountains were at least a hundred miles away even though they looked much closer and the thief had about a six hour start, riding a fresh horse. It was obvious the man knew where he was going from the straight trail he left. If he were to catch up with him he would have to ride hard and save the horse as much as possible. They had ridden about two hours now and Breathtaker had discontinued his frolicking and playing and cantered along beside the big bay easily. Breathtaker was in top racing condition and could do that for a long time before he tired out. It was the big bay Jess was riding that he had to worry about. Jess noticed from the tracks that the rider had slowed considerably. Probably saving his horse, thought Jess, as they continued their pace.

The early June sun was bearing down now and Jess knew that it would not be long before darkness fell upon the desert and he would need to stop and make camp for the night. Off to the southwest there was a dark thunder head that looked as though it could produce some rain. As Jess rode on he kept an eye on the cloud and it intensified rapidly. Jess could see that it extended down to the horizon and at the base there seemed to be a dark orange cast like nothing he had seen before. He continued to watch the oncoming storm and after a few minutes he knew what the dark orange color was. It was sand, and a mighty sand storm it was. He started looking for a place to serve as shelter from the oncoming storm but there was nothing. The wind was now picking up and a drop of rain could be felt now and again. Jess slid off his horse and pulled the two horses close together and got between their heads and held them firmly with their rear end toward the oncoming storm. Suddenly the wind began to whistle and thrash the desert sage and a choking dust surrounded them. The flying sand burned his neck and ears and the horses humped their backs and stood still with their ears laid flat against their head. Now and again Jess could hear above the roar of the wind the horses coughing and blowing the dust and sand from their nostrils. The burning winds continued for twenty minutes or more and Jess knew that if the wind continued much longer his bared skin would be bleeding. The blowing sand felt as though he was being stuck with a million needles and it burned as it dug at his skin as the fierce wind howled. It burned like hell, that sand, and there seemed to be no end to the torture. Tumble- weeds rushed by, some rolling underneath the horse, but they didn't care. Jess held his hat firmly with his left hand while he held the horses with his right. Suddenly, the wind began to lay and the darkness of the storm was replaced with light and Jess knew the hellish ordeal was about over.

After the storm had subsided, Jess tried to brush the sand from the saddle and realized that he would have to remove and re-saddle the horse. Jess finished shaking the sand from the blankets, re-saddled the horse and mounted up. Suddenly there was something terribly wrong... There was no trail... The wind had erased every trace. A slight panic came over him. It would be a guess now, and to, there were also no tracks back the way he had come. There was a flicker of panic and Jess realized that he would be lost out in the middle of that hellish desert. He calmed himself . . . He had to think now . . . He had to keep his head and not panic. Suddenly he remembered that before the storm the trail was leading directly toward a tall, distant peak that extended high above the horizon. He looked around and there it was. He stepped in the stirrup and mounted then pointed his mount in the direction of the peak and pushed on. He rode on for an hour or so, knowing that he must find a place to make camp for the night, he pulled up and surveyed the landscape once again, taking time to look behind him and get his bearings. He needed rest and both the horses needed the rest after the long day's ride. As he rode on, he remembered a movie that John Wayne had made and Jess suddenly knew the trip the cowboy had made across the hot waste lands in that movie was not exactly the same, but it reminded him of the scene. The big difference was, he was no John Wayne and, moreover, his jeans had lots of sand in them and the grit was playing hell with his rear end. Yes, this trip was the real thing.

The late evening sun had now gone down, casting a beautiful amber glow in the big country to the west. There was no trail now and no signs to indicate whether the thief was walking his horse or if he had even changed direction. Jess knew that it would be only a matter of time before the thief would stop and rest for the night. After all, he was in the same shape that Jess was in; both he and his horse would be tired.

It was getting late now and darkness would come within a couple of hours. The landscape had changed and there were large sand dunes scattered across the desert floor. Barrel cactus and Spanish bayonets dotted the landscape. The only problem was, there was no water for the horses. Jess rode up to a grove of mesquite and dismounted to unsaddle the bay. The trail had been easy to follow before the storm but he had continued toward the tall mountain peak. In the distance, maybe a half hour ride more, there seemed to be an image of a stand of low growing timber. Trees? Growing out here in the middle of the desert? Suddenly Jess thought about what the fat lawman had said about the water and knew that there must be a water hole up ahead. There had to be water for timber to be growing. Jess tightened the saddle girth again, mounted and rode on at a slow canter toward the timber. After he had ridden for a few minutes the timber became more distinct and he knew there was water. Suddenly he had a strange feeling come over him. Something didn't seem quite right and he pulled up the horse to try to sort things out. They were now within about a mile of the trees and suddenly Jess realized he could be riding into another ambush and thought about the bullet that had creased his head two days before and how sore it was. He scanned the landscape carefully, looking for any kind of protection. There were several fairly tall sand dunes off to his right about a quarter of a mile and he could tell that they continued on and were fairly in line with the water hole. The last one looked to be near the timber and if that were the case he could use it for cover. He pulled the bay off what he believed to be the trail and headed for the sand dunes. He kept the dunes between him and the trees for protection, riding from one to the other until he was nearing the last of the series of dunes. He pulled up the bay near the last one, dismounted, and started to lead the horses to the edge of the dune for a better look at the timber. No sooner than he took a step, a rifle cracked and the screaming bullet hit the right brim of his hat. Jess fell to the ground and took cover behind the bay. He pushed the horse toward the nearby sand dunes for cover. The rifle cracked again and the screaming bullet hit just behind Breathtaker kicking up sand. Breathtaker lunged forward pulling the bay and Jess along with him. His sudden lunge pulled them behind the sand dune out of the thief's line of sight. Jess quickly cut two pieces of the cotton rope and hobbled the horses so that they couldn't run off. The last thing he needed was to be in the middle of a Mexican desert on foot. He pulled the rifle out of the holster and kicked out the empty hull and pushed another into the chamber while climbing in a forward crouched position to the crest of the sand dune. Jess eased the rifle over the crest and attempted to sneak a look toward the water hole. Suddenly a shot rang out and then three more in succession. All of the bullets hit just in front of him, sand blasting him with sand every round. Jess eased back a few feet down the sand dune and lay still thinking about the situation. Suddenly he spoke out loud.

"I've heard of a Mexican stand off all my life and now I've been in two in three days. What the hell do I do now?" he said out loud.

He continued to lie still for a while and then eased his rifle barrel up extending it above the crest. Again, four or five shots rang out, the bullets screaming overhead. Jess hadn't been keeping count of the shots but he knew that there must have been twenty at least. He laid thinking about what he must do for a full ten minutes. Darkness was coming fast now, so he eased his head up and peeped over the crest of the sand once again but this time no shots were fired. He lay still for a minute then eased his head up a little higher over the crest so that he could get a better look. Everything seemed quiet at the water hole and he could see no movement. He scanned the desert to the east of the water hole. He couldn't see any sign of movement. He looked just west of the water hole and made out the dim image of a rider, riding hard toward the distant mountain range. The thief had slipped out, using the trees as cover until he was out of rifle range, and then he had continued his course toward the mountains. Jess knew that he could not go very far riding hard like that. The horse was tired and would either break down or he would be forced to stop for the night to let his horse rest. Jess un-hobbled the horses and rode in to the water hole. As he rode up to the place where the firing had come from, there lay a Winchester rifle with the lever pulled back and the chamber open. There were the spent bullet hulls and an empty cartridge box lying off to the side.

"So that's it! The jasper is out of bullets and has left the rifle to lighten his load." Jess whispered and led the horses down to the edge of the water hole and let them drink hard and deep from the pool. After they had drunk, he unsaddled the bay and let him roll, then picketed the horses near the water hole in deep grass for the night. There was plenty of fire wood around under the trees so Jess dragged up a sizable pile of dried limbs then started a small fire. He took the bedroll from the saddle and suddenly the thought hit him. If he made his bed there by the fire, he would be a sitting duck and easy picking for the thief, if he decided to back track. He sure didn't need to be an easy target so he carried the saddle and bedroll back into the dark shadows of the trees, and then rolled it out. The fire was going now so Jess dipped up a pot of water from the pool, poured a half hand full of coffee into the water, and set it on the fire to boil. He reached in his pocket and pulled out the Swiss army knife that Susan had given him for a birthday present and opened a can of beans. It would be beans, canned sausages, and coffee for supper and right then he was ready for it. After he had cleaned up the grub, he poured himself a cup of the boiled coffee and leaned back against a fallen log near the fire. As he sat sipping on the hot coffee, Jess watched the horses nipping large bites of the rich, green grass that grew around the water hole. Breathtaker would eat for a while and then lift his head and look around surveying the sounds of the night crickets, frogs and insects around the water hole. He had been stalled for a long time while in training and he was enjoying the freedom of the outdoors. As Jess sat thinking about what he would do next to catch the thief, he wondered if the man had another weapon. Maybe he did but why would he have run so quickly if he did? Jess thought about that for a while and then walked out to where Breathtaker was grazing and began to pet him and talk. Jess stood watching the young horse as he vigorously nibbled on the lush water grass and it made sense to believe that the man had only the one gun or he would have stayed and made his stand there at the water hole. He had cover from the timber, water to drink and there was no other cover until he reached the distant mountains. Jess petted Breathtaker on the neck and began to speak.

"You big gray devil, it's up to you now . . . I reckon the bay is plumb tuckered out from the hard ride."

The light was leaving fast, especially around the water hole in the shadows. Jess gathered some additional dead branches for fire and added them to the pile. He walked back into the shadows and spread the saddle blanket upside down on top of the saddle so that it would dry over night and lay down on his bed roll. He noticed one of the saddle bags was spilling oats and realized that the old rancher had filled both saddle bags with oats for the horses. He walked back out to where the horses were grazing and poured the grain out in two small piles on the ground for them. It wasn't a full feeding of oats but it was enough to keep their strength up for a hard ride tomorrow and he was grateful to the old rancher.

After Jess fed the horses the grain, he sat looking into the fire. He thought about the thief and wondered just how far the crazy fool would try to make it before he let the horse rest.

The fire flickered and cracked as he sat staring into it. The flame would seem to go completely out and then suddenly flicker back up again as it diminished and burned the remaining fuel of the wood down to a glow of amber coals. Jess got up from where he was sitting and walked out to where he could see in the direction the thief had taken. He climbed to the crest of a large sand dune. In the distance he could barely make out the glow of a small fire, far out in the desert, and knew that the thief had been forced to stop. "Oh, yes! He's out of ammo," said Jess, talking to himself.

Jess turned and started walking back toward the fire. He knew even if he had seen the fire, the thief might have come back and for all he knew might be lying somewhere close now just waiting for him to go to sleep. He walked back to the shadows, pulled his boots off and lay down on the bedroll he had spread next to his saddle. He pulled the Winchester out of the sheath and leaned it up against the saddle, close enough that he could reach it easily. He placed the .38 on his stomach and stretched out with his right hand on the gun As he lay there watching the flickering fire some thirty feet away, he thought about what he must do in order to catch the thief.

    Jess thought about the desert country he was in and the Government of Mexico and he wondered if there had ever been good law enforcement anywhere south of the Border. His knowledge of Mexican history was weak but it was not because he did not have a desire to know, there was just not much taught in school about our neighbors to the south. Of course, there was a lot taught about the great T'ang dynasty that rose up in China and other far away places or some other un-interesting civilization or government. He thought about ancient history and how some of the civilizations that had sprung up over time and for some unknown reason only faded away, leaving little for modern man to learn about them. He lay for a long time and his thoughts turned to home and his soft bed and he wished he was there with Susan. He was tired, really tired, but he knew he needed to stay awake. There was danger out there and it could mean life or maybe sudden death if he slept. His mind swirled and he was overcome, collapsing from fatigue. He faded into a deep sleep. He was not sure how long he had been asleep when his eyes popped wide open. A sound, he thought. He lay there still. He was unsure what kind of sound had woken him, but it was a sound, he knew that for sure. It had to be a sound that woke him up. He lay motionless, afraid to even bat his eyes.

Suddenly a dry twig snapped of to his left and a cold chill crawled up his backbone and settled at the back of his neck and he froze. He knew that he dared not to reach for the rifle. It was too risky. His hand was on the .38 but the thief probably had him in his sights then, just waiting for him to move. Jess knew that he had to manage to get some kind of an advantage. It was the thief . . . He had come back to finish him off and he would do it. Foolishly he'd slept and he had made a big mistake . . . A fatal mistake . . . He was caught sleeping. He ever so slowly stretched his fingers around the .38 and continued to be still, even though he didn't hear the sound or hear anything moving about. He knew someone or something was near the water hole, and moreover, he knew he was in grave danger. His heart was pounding a mile a minute. Suddenly Jess heard something lapping the water and knew it was some kind of wild animal. He sat up quickly and pointed the .38 in the direction of the sound. Just as suddenly through the dim light of the fire he saw an antelope as it lunged away from the water hole and dashed off into the desert. Jess lay back down, relieved but shaken, and he contemplated on that for a while. That was the way it was in the old times. A man had to sleep light on the trail in order to stay alive, that was for sure. Jess looked at his watch and could barely make out the time in the dim glow of the fading fire. It was 2:00 a.m. and he needed sleep. He lay for a while thinking about the shooting at the livery stable. His eyes closed and he again fell asleep.

Chapter 15

Jess sat up suddenly, flicked his lighter so he could see, and took a look at his watch. It was now five o'clock. He put his hat on and shook his boots to assure himself there wasn't a scorpion or snake inside them before he pulled them on. He got up and placed an armload of dead branches where the fire had been and rekindled it to heat the coffee. As he sat drinking the strong coffee, his mind drifted back to a time when the old cowboys pushed the vast herds of longhorns up the north trail. He imagined that some of them had done exactly the same thing at some point in time along the trail. He also knew that some of them must have experienced a scary moment like his during the night.

It had been a dark night and there had been no moon to light the desert. Jess knew the thief likely had stayed the night where he had seen the fire, but he also knew that he would move out at early light. It was a full hour before daylight now and he could make out the image of the horses from the glow of the fire. He finished his second cup of coffee and walked out to where Breathtaker stood dozing with one back foot cocked. He knew that Breathtaker had rested and grazed all night and he would be fresh again. He removed Breathtaker's halter and hung it over his shoulder, forced the snaffle bit into the young stallion's mouth and slipped the one-ear head stall over the colt's sleek fox ears. Jess led Breathtaker to the fire and rubbed him down with the Mexican saddle blanket that had now fully dried during the night. He saddled the young horse and tied him to a small tree near the water. Jess left the bay picketed to stay behind and graze until he came back by later in the day. He took the remaining coffee that was in the pot and doused it on the fire. He checked the shells in the Winchester just to be sure and then slipped it into the saddle sheath. Jess led Breathtaker out of the trees to a clear spot, stepped in the stirrup and mounted. Breathtaker pranced and Jess began to talk to him.

"You gray devil, this is the first time I've ever sat on your young back and I'll say one thing. You are one fine hunk of horseflesh," stated Jess, as he talked to the big, gray colt and petted him on the neck.

Jess pointed the colt northwest and rode cautiously through the cactus and scattered sand dunes in the gray, early morning dawn. Out about a quarter of a mile to the south, a coyote scampered down the side of a sand dune trying to catch a field mouse. In the early morning dawn four distant antelope watched Breathtaker and his rider cautiously. The dim glow of the thief's fire up ahead grew brighter now and it was evident the thief had re-kindled it. Jess knew that he was still there. As the early desert light began to move across the wasteland, Jess kept the cover of the sand dunes between him and the camp fire as much as possible until he got to within about two hundred yards of the small fire. It was now getting light enough to see a little and suddenly Breathtaker's head come up and his ears flicked forward. Jess knew Breathtaker had seen something and Jess then made out the silhouette of a horse and rider leaving the fire heading toward the mountains. Breathtaker pranced and pulled at the bit wanting to run. Jess just hoped Breathtaker didn't nicker to the other horse, so he kept talking to him.

"Hold on, boy, settle down," whispered Jess. "We've got plenty of time, let's get a little closer and then we're going to have us a 'thief catch'n out here in the middle of the Mexican desert this morning." He patted the big gray colt on the neck and continued to whisper to him for reassurance, hoping the colt wouldn't call to the horse up ahead. Breathtaker pulled at the bit with his ears erect, watching the horse and rider closely. From his training, Breathtaker knew that he was supposed to catch the front horse. Jess nudged him with his heel and eased him into a short canter. Breathtaker bowed his neck and pulled at the bit as they quickly closed ground on the horse and rider up ahead. The landscape had changed now and the desert floor was fairly level, with little or no vegetation. Jess Steel could feel his heart hammering against his chest and he and Breathtaker both knew the race was about to begin. He just hoped the thief didn't have a hand gun. They were now within about fifty yards of the horse and rider. Suddenly, the thief looked back over his shoulder and saw them coming. Instantly he spurred his horse into a full run. Jess took a deep seat and screamed out at Breathtaker and let him have his head. Breathtaker almost ran out from under Jess and in one mighty leap he was running at top speed. With every mighty stride the colt gained ground on the sorrel horse up ahead. Jess couldn't believe the power and speed of his mount and suddenly he knew that he was mounted on the best horse that he had ever ridden in his entire life. Breathtaker darted through the sparse cactus and desert sage and was fast closing ground. To Breathtaker this was just another horse race and Jess knew the colt was enjoying every powerful stride of it. He reached out and slapped him lightly on the neck and began to talk to him.

"Come on colt, let's take him now. I always wanted to be a rodeo bull-dog artist," Jess's heart pounded with excitement. Breathtaker pinned his ears and responded with a burst of speed that carried them to within four lengths of the fugitive. Jess could now hear the thief's mount breathing hard and knew the horse was pretty much used up. It was for sure the thief didn't have a hand gun or he would have been shooting by now. Jess reached back and pulled the Winchester out of the sheath and held it firmly in his right hand just in case he needed it. Breathtaker was now within two lengths of the horse and rider, running hard, going after the lead with his ears pinned flat against his head. Suddenly Jess saw the thief reach for his knife and begin to slash the air wildly. Breathtaker surged forward. Jess knew that he needed to stay clear of the thief's slashing knife at all costs. He didn't need to get a nasty cut, especially out there in the middle of the desert. Just as Breathtaker was about ready to pass the other horse, Jess brought the rifle barrel down hard across the thief's back, knocking him loose from the saddle and sending him sailing through the air. Jess stood in the stirrups and slowed the colt but Breathtaker didn't have a very good stop. He was trained to run on the track so Jess made a large circle then turned him back toward the man now sprawled motionless on the ground. As Jess pulled up, he stepped down and cautiously punched the Mexican with the muzzle of his rifle. There was no movement. He was out cold. With the piece of rope that he had used to hobble Breathtaker, he tied the thief's hands firmly together behind his back and then doused him good with water from the canteen. The Mexican opened his eyes and tried to scramble away but Jess pinned him firmly with his right foot against his man's chest. Jess held the muzzle of the Winchester not more than four inches from the thief's nose. The scared Mexican began shaking his head from side to side.

"No kill policia! No kill policia! No! No!"

Jess's blood ran cold. There attached to the killer's waist was the pouch containing the money. "Yeah, you low down sucker, you just told off on your self. You did kill Emanuel, that's for sure now and what I should do is blow your damn head off right out here in the middle of this desert and leave you for the buzzards to pick. That's exactly what I should do. Now get your sorry butt up from there," said Jess, as he pushed him hard with his foot. The Mexican scrambled to his feet and Jess pointed the way they had come, motioning with the muzzle of the Winchester.

Jess was mad. "Now you walk, damn you! If you make a false move I'll blow the back of your damn head off,"

The stolen horse, stood off to Jess's left a few feet still breathing heavily from the run. Jess caught up the horse, gathered up the reins, then tied them together and hung them on his saddle horn. Jess knew the horse would have followed. He was too tired to run away. Breathtaker was walking slowly behind Jess now but he showed little sign of hard breathing. The gray colt extended his head out and pushed Jess forward with his nose.

"Just hang on, boy, we're headed that way. You're thinking about those oats, that's your problem." The Mexican looked back over his shoulder at Jess in disgust and hissed profanity. Jess couldn't understand the language but knew in his own mind that he was cursing.

Jess prodded the killer in the back with the muzzle of the rifle. "Turn around and keep walking."

They had now walked about a half mile and Jess determined that Breathtaker had it much too easy and besides, his right boot was hurting his foot. Jess stepped in the stirrup, lifted his leg over the saddle and petted the colt on the neck. Breathtaker now was walking close behind the killer. He was crowding him, gaining ground, forcing the man to move faster. He reached out with his nose just as he had done Jess and he pushed the killer forward. The killer stumbled and looked back over his shoulder at Breathtaker and frowned.

Jess laughed and petted Breathtaker on the neck. "That's the way boy. Show him which way to go. If he looks back again push his ass down on the ground and step on him if you want to."

After about an hour of walking, they made it back to the water hole. Jess pulled the saddle off of the horse the Mexican had been riding and saddled the bay. After helping the killer up into the saddle, he tied a slip loop in the cotton rope and put it over the killer's head and around his neck. The other end of the rope he then dallied to his own saddle horn. The killer had a disgusted look on his face and rolled out a line of Spanish. Jess did not understand a thing he said but had a sneaky feeling that he was being cursed a lot.

Jess motioned with the Winchester for the killer to move out. "Go ahead and run your mouth. All you've got to do now is try and run off anytime you think you want too. I'll assure one thing, when you hit the end of that rope, it'll stretch your neck about twice the length it is now." Breathtaker walked out behind the killer toward the old rancher's place. Jess kept a little slack in the rope so that if the killer decided to lunge his horse, there would be a sudden stop when the killer hit the end of the rope.

As they rode on, Breathtaker had a little quick spring in his walk and Jess could feel the colt's muscles working under him. Jess thought about what a good horse he was and suddenly the thought hit him not to race Breathtaker anymore for fear of getting him crippled. He knew that would be a waste. After all, he was born to be a race horse. He *was* a racehorse, a good one and he liked to run. Well, at least they could enter him in a few allowance races that had a good purse and maybe his winnings would help offset the feed cost for the brood mare band. Jess knew for sure that Breathtaker was going to hang around as his breeding stallion. Why in the world would he want to send mares to those high-dollar breeding farms to get them bred when he had a first-class race horse in his own barn? Yes, Breathtaker would be his stallion and perhaps produce some more foals that could run like their sire.

Chapter 16

As the sun settled behind the blue-hazed mountains over his right shoulder, the entire western sky cast a soft glow of pastel shades of amber that framed the picturesque, dun landscape. Now and again Jess saw small birds with brilliant yellow breasts fluttering in and out of the cacti. They would hop here and there searching for food while looking for a place to roost for the night. The desert had a special kind of beauty but Jess Steel had seen about all the strange beauty he could stand. He was ready to take Breathtaker and go to Oklahoma. Earlier in the day, they had ridden up on a rattlesnake and Jess had to shoot it with the Winchester to keep Breathtaker from throwing him. It had been a long day of riding but Jess took it slow and they rode at a walk most of the day. Jess knew there was no need to tire the horses any more than they already were by pushing on and too Breathtaker was just a two-year-old. It was still a good half day's ride to the old rancher's place so Jess began to look for a place to camp for the night. There wasn't much out there to use for fueling a camp fire, but Jess finally picked a spot that had several dead barrel cactus. Jess rode up along side the killer and checked the rope around the killer's wrist to make sure it was still secure. He lifted the rope from around the killer's neck and motioned for him to get down. The Mexican jumped to the ground and then sat down and was sullen. He watched Jess as he dragged the dead cactus up with the rope. Jess knew the killer would take any opportunity to get away during the night so he left him tied up. Jess started to tie the long rope around one of the killer's feet and suddenly the killer kicked Jess in the face and hissed Mexican profanity. Jess's face ran hot with anger and blood trickled from the corner of his mouth from a busted lip. He slapped the man hard across the face with his right hand and pushed him over in the sand with his foot. The killer continued to mumble and hiss at Jess.

"That's all right, just go ahead and blow, you sorry piece of humanity. With Tony's money and down here in Mexico, I wouldn't give two cents for your stinking hide. They'll likely line you up against a rock wall and fill you with hot lead for killing a policeman, I suspect."

Jess shoved the killer down onto the ground again with his right foot and held him firmly as he tied the rope securely to the killer's leg. Jess knew he was in for a sleepless night. He would take no chance of the killer escaping, and he knew if the killer got his hands on the rifle he would be a dead man. Before lying down for the night, Jess planned to secure the rope to his own arm and keep the rope tight so if the killer moved during the night, he would feel the tug from the rope.

Jess tossed the rope to the side then spread out the bedroll, pulled out the last can of pork-n-beans and opened it with his knife. The Mexican watched him with hungry eyes as he opened the beans, so Jess took a strip of the jerky and walked over and stuck it into the killer's mouth.

"Here . . . Chew on that . . . That may be a little tough without the use of your hands but do the best you can. Anyway, that's all you get and if you drop it that's your problem. This is no Sunday picnic and I shouldn't even give you that much. If the horses can go without water and feed tonight, so can you," snarled Jess.

Jess leaned back against Breathtaker's saddle and ate the pork-n-beans and watched the hungry Mexican as he wrestled with the strip of beef jerky.

After Jess finished his beans and canned sausage he unsaddled the horses and piled up some of the dry cactus and started a fire. He kept the fire small in order to save fuel but it made decent light to see by. Jess also knew the fire would help to keep the scorpions and rattlers out of the area as well. The pile of dried cactus that he had gathered would need to last until daylight. The Mexican sat watching him without expression. Jess knew that the killer was tired and thirsty. He had not had a drink of water since they left the water hole and he really didn't care. Anybody that would kill a man in cold blood like he did should starve to death, thought Jess.

Finally during the night the killer dozed off and then leaned over and fell asleep. Jess kept the fire going all night and at five o'clock he poured some water from the canteen and boiled a pot of coffee. After his usual three cups of the strong coffee, he jerked the rope hard and watched the startled, sleepy Mexican as he sat up quickly. Jess walked over and untied the rope from the killer's leg. This time the killer had no kick in him but Jess watched him closely just to be sure. Jess saddled the sorrel gelding for the killer and motioned for him to mount up. The killer just stood there sullen. Jess caught the Mexican by the seat of the pants and practically threw him up on the horse. Then he tightened the synch strap on Breathtaker's saddle.

It was early when Jess stepped into the stirrup and mounted Breathtaker that morning. A gray dawn lay across the desert floor and the desert seemed to have no end. Jess Steel slipped the rope over the killers head just as he had done the day before. He motioned with the Winchester to move out and then nudged Breathtaker with his right boot. Breathtaker wasn't so fresh now. He needed a drink of water and the trail was beginning to wear on him a little. Jess kept the killer in front of him all morning as they rode on. Jess looked at his watch and it was now ten o'clock. Far up ahead, he could barely make out the image of the old rancher's barn and the squeaking windmill in the distance. He knew they would be there within an hour and it couldn't be too soon to suit him. They rode on for a while and then through weary, sleepless eyes Jess could make out the image of the fat policeman and the old rancher standing near the house waiting. As they rode up, the fat lawman and the old rancher met them.

"*Señor, we now believe the man you have captured to be the killer,*" said the fat policeman.

Jess untied the rope from his saddle horn and tossed it to the policeman. "Well, I'm glad you had time to think about it and that you've had a change of heart, because he's damn sure the killer." Jess was totally disgusted with the lazy lawman's statement. The lawman continued to jabber about what he believed to be fact and then Jess couldn't take it any more.

"Well, if you will shut up your fat, lazy mouth, I'll tell you what I know to be fact . . . Now this is what he said, so just listen." Jess was tired and irritated.

Jess told him what the killer had said after he had run him down and then Jess pointed to the money pouch. "There's your proof, that's the money that Emanuel had on him when he was shot."

"*Señor, you have gained a reward of 250,000 pesos for his capture. Emanuel's father posted the reward yesterday in hopes that someone would catch him so that we can give him true justice for killing a policia.*"

Jess patted Breathtaker on the neck and began unsaddling him. The rancher led all the horses to the water trough and let them drink from the clear, cool water being pumped by the noisy windmill. After they had finished drinking, the rancher came over to where Jess sat in the shade of the horse trailer. The old man reached out and shook Jess's hand. *"Mucho gracias, Señor."*

As the fat policeman sped away with the killer in

his police car, Jess relaxed for the first time in three days. He was glad it was all over. He felt good about catching the man who had killed his friend and all that he needed now was to get some sleep, collect the reward money, and take Breathtaker home.

The old rancher led the two horses along with Breathtaker into the barn and put them in a stall with grain and plenty of hay and water. Jess spread the bedroll in the shade of the trailer and took a long, much needed nap. Late in the afternoon he was awakened by the rancher. The old man waited until Jess got himself awake and then pointed to a small makeshift table that he had set near the trailer. While Jess was asleep, he had prepared a large meal of beef tacos, with beans and rice.

"No Chile! No Chile," stated the old man, as he chuckled and continued to smile through the long handle-bar mustache.

Jess suddenly remembered the hot peppers that he and Emanuel had experienced at the livery stable four days ago and knew the old man was telling him the food was not that hot.

The two men sat down at the table and with no conversation they ate their fill of the good food. After they had finished, Jess got up from the table and shook the old man's hand.

"Gracias, Señor," he said as he tipped his hat and walked to the truck. It was time to collect the reward money. He had no intention of keeping it but knew if he didn't collect, it would somehow disappear. Someone would collect it and it would likely be the fat policeman.

Jess entered the police station and was greeted by the fat Mexican policeman.

"I see the hero of the day has come to make arrangements for the reward money."

"Yes. What do I need to do?"

"*Señor, it is only a matter of signing this form, then we can go to the bank and your money will be transferred here to you or to your bank in the United States, whichever you wish,*" said the policeman.

"Oh, it must be sent to my bank in Oklahoma." Jess knew that if word got out that he was carrying that kind of money on him in Mexico he would probably be dead within twenty minutes.

The policeman hopped up from his chair. *"Come. We will go to the bank. We must hurry for it will close in ten minutes."* As they walked down the street to the bank Jess asked the policeman to go with him out to the rancher's house and translate for him.

"I want to leave Breathtaker with the rancher and return to Juarez and visit with Tony for a day or two. I think the old man will take good care of my horse but he needs to know what I plan to do and that I am willing to pay him for his efforts," said Jess.

"Si, Señor, I will tell him but he will likely not accept your payment. He feels indebted to you for bringing him his horse that was stolen. As soon as we finish, we will go there."

After they had conducted the business, Jess used the police department's telephone to make a collect call home. He talked to Susan for a long time assuring her that he was all right and that nothing had happened to him. He told her about his policeman friend being killed and that he had caught the killer. After talking to Susan, he called the barn and talked to Alex.

"Alex, I've got him back just like I told you I would," said Jess.

Jess heard Alex yell with excitement. Jess knew that Alex would be staying late at the barn in hope of a call from him. Susan told him Alex had stayed late every night since he had left.

"Alex, make arrangements for someone to feed for

you for three or four days and then get with Susan and you all make plans to come pick up Breathtaker. I'll meet you all in El Paso with him day after tomorrow at the airport. I'll try to make my truck conspicuous so it will be easy to find. I'll be pulling our trailer, so look for it. I won't go into that, it's a long story and I'll tell you all about it when you get here. Susan and I will be staying here for a few days. I need to attend a funeral here Sunday and I'm sure Susan will want to look around and do a little shopping afterward. We haven't had a vacation in a long time so if Susan wants to we may just look around out here some before coming home. Breathtaker's in good shape so come get him and take him home and turn him out into a paddock and let him rest and just be a horse for a while."

"Jess, we'll leave out tomorrow and see you in El Paso at about, say, ten o'clock, day after tomorrow," said Alex, as he said goodbye and hung up the telephone.

It was getting pretty dark when Jess and the policeman pulled up at the rancher's place and got out. The man met them on the porch carrying a lantern in his left hand that cast dim, amber light across the porch. In his right hand he carried the Winchester. The policeman spoke to him and the Mexican rancher sat down and motioned for them to take a seat. Jess began telling the policeman what he wanted him to say. "Tell him that I will be going to Juarez tonight and I would like him to keep my horse and take care of him while I am gone. Tell him that I will pick him up tomorrow and I will pay him two hundred pesos for feed and his inconvenience".

The policeman spoke to the old rancher and told him what Jess wanted him to do, then, he turned to Jess. *"He said that would be agreeable Señor, but says that he will not accept the money."*

"Tell him that I want him to have the money and also tell him to watch closely and not let anyone steal Breathtaker while I am gone."

The policeman told him what Jess had said. The old man turned and looked straight at Jess through tired eyes and then laid his withered hand on the side the Winchester and nodded at Jess.

"Si, Señor."

Chapter 17

Jess pulled the Ford diesel up in front of Tony's house and then turned off the engine. He sat in the truck for a little while thinking about what he should say to Tony. This was going to be really difficult. What can you say to someone who's lost a son? Jess got out and walked up to the door and rang the bell. An older woman opened the door. Jess removed his hat and spoke to the woman. "I'm Jess Steel; I wanted to pay my respects to the family."

"Si, Señor Steel, we have been expecting you. I am the mother of Emanuel's wife. Come, I will take you to Tony now."

As they walked into the large living room, Tony met Jess with an outstretched hand and then he placed an arm on Jess's shoulder and shook his head as grief gripped him to the depths of his soul.

Tony wiped his eyes with his handkerchief. *"Amigo, it is very hard to lose a son such as mine. It is a heartbreaking thing. I have relived my life with him many times in the past four days and cannot understand why he had to be taken from us so soon. He was a good man."*

"Yes, Tony." Emanuel was a very good man and a brave man. I just want you to know that you have my deepest sympathy." Jess stared at the floor searching for words.

"For what it's worth, Tony, I did run the man down in the desert and the thief who committed this horrible crime is securely locked away."

"I knew that you had run him down with your fast horse and captured him. The policia called me and told me that he was behind bars and what you had done to bring him in. I am grateful to you for your dangerous efforts. Did you get the reward?"

"Yes, I got the reward, but when my wife gets here I will give you a check for the amount. I do not want the reward, Tony. I only took it, believing that the policeman there would get it if I didn't. I had it transferred to my account in Oklahoma. I sure didn't want to carry that amount of money around with me until I saw you."

"The money will stay in Oklahoma. It is yours and you will keep it."

"But Tony, I would not feel right taking the reward since we were looking for my horse at the time Emanuel was. . . " Jess stopped short.

"Well, Amigo, the money will go to the great racing horse that ran down the killer and that is my final word on the matter. If you and your horse had not been here the killer would never have been caught and would never be brought to the justice that he deserves. There is no more to be said,"

Jess was at a loss for words and felt as though he was committing some sort of crime by taking the reward, so he changed the subject and knew that he would address it later.

"I must go secure the necessary paperwork in order to get Breathtaker back across the border."

"I will go with you, Jess Steel. You will not know where to go and will not be able to speak to them."

"Oh, I appreciate you volunteering to help Tony, but I could not ask you to go, that would not be right," said Jess.

"It will be exactly right. I need to get out for a while. It will do me good. I know exactly where to go and we will get everything taken care of very quickly, Amigo."

Tony got his hat and the two men were off to secure the necessary paperwork.

As they traveled Jess told Tony that Susan and Alex were coming down and would be there within two days. He told him that Alex would take Breathtaker home and Susan would stay with him to attend the funeral.

"That is good, Amigo, that she is coming, I know that she must be a wonderful woman and I look forward to meeting her. I will be delighted that she is here. You will stay at my casa while she is here and that will help to occupy my aching mind."

"We will be happy to stay, but we do not want to create a hardship for you are your family during your time of grief."

"It will not be a hardship and I will be pleased that you are here," Tony insisted.

"Susan will likely want to spend an extra day and shop at some of the markets in Juarez before going home."

"That is good. I own three large markets here as do two of my cousins. She will find many things that she will like."

After they had completed the business of getting paperwork to get the horses back across the border Tony asked, *"When are you going to get your racing horse, Amigo?"*

"I am supposed to meet Alex and Susan day after tomorrow at the El Paso airport with Breathtaker. Alex is coming down here to pick up the horse and then he will leave immediately going back to Oklahoma."

"If you don't mind, I would like to go with you to pick up your horse, Amigo. The ride will be good for me and I am anxious to see this horse you call Breathtaker."

Jess had a feeling that Tony was a little afraid for him to go back to get the horse alone and Jess looked forward to his company. It would make the time pass much faster and also Tony could talk for him.

"Do you still have the weapon that Emanuel gave to you?"

Jess took a quick glance at Tony out of the corner of his eye. "Oh, yes, I still have the weapon and my boot gun as well,"

Tony didn't make any comment to Jess's answer. A thought flashed through Jess's mind and he wondered if Tony had it in his mind to try and do away with the killer? Or, maybe he just wants a gun for protection. The thought made Jess feel a little uneasy. That's all he needed now was to get tangled up in a killing like that.

"Tony, what will happen to the killer? How does the Mexican law work down here?"

"He will be given the harshest of sentences, a sentence of death by the firing squad, and I shall be there to watch him die."

Jess sat silent for a while and then candidly looked at Tony. "Tony, I almost blew the back of his head off out there in the desert. I could have, you know, and no one would have ever known. Now I'm glad I didn't. Sometimes a man's temper will make him do things that he will be sorry for later on."

"I could kill him and never bat an eye but that would be much too easy. I want him to wait and to know what is going to happen. I want him to wait for the bullet to hit him. I want him to cry from fear and lose control of his bladder just before he dies. That is what I want to see."

That put Jess's mind at ease. At least Tony wasn't planning to kill him while he was in jail.

"Why did you ask about the weapon?"

"No particular reason other than I do not like to leave home over night without protection of some kind. There are some men that will kill for five pesos. Especially if they think that you have something they can steal. I had a very good friend that left Juarez for the weekend and headed down south to buy some leather goods from a

saddle maker. He never showed up again nor has his body been found. I am sure that he was carrying some money on him to buy the goods. Some one probably saw the money then waited until he was alone then killed him. One never knows who is watching and who is capable of committing crimes of that nature down here."

Jess turned the truck into the driveway at Tony's house and pulled to a stop. "Well, Tony, if you want to go with me to get Breathtaker we should leave soon if we are to get down there before dark. It's about a five hour drive. Do you have a sleeping bag?"

Tony opened the truck door and slid out of the seat. *"Yes, I have one and I will get some things and we will leave immediately."*

Jess waited in the truck and after Tony returned, they were off to get Breathtaker. Jess wondered how Breathtaker was doing and if he was sore after the long ride. They rode south for a long while and came upon the cantina where he and Emanuel had stopped. Jess wondered if Falena was still there but he did not say a word about the incident to Tony. He just drove on as if the cantina didn't exist.

"Do you know a place where we can sleep tonight?" asked Tony.

"We can sleep at the old rancher's place. I noticed a nice haystack in the barn and I'm sure we will be welcome to stay there for the night," said Jess, as they sped on southward.

"That is good. I am not accustomed to sleeping in a haystack but did not like the thought of staying near the village. We are strangers there and we would not be safe. Yes, the haystack will be fine."

Jess slowed the truck as they entered the village and then turned off onto the gravel road leading out of town toward the rancher's place. As they turned into the long drive leading up to the house it was getting late and almost dark. Jess could see the amber-glowing window brightened by the lantern inside. As they pulled up to a stop the man appeared on the porch holding the lantern in his left hand and the Winchester in his right. "Speak to him, Tony, let him know that it is me and introduce your self to him. He is a good man but I believe he could be a little salty," said Jess.

Tony called out to him in Spanish just as Jess had suggested. The man motioned for them to approach and then invited them to sit down on the porch. Tony began to talk to the man in Spanish. They talked for a long time and then the rancher stood up and stepped off of the porch and led the way to the barn and showed them where they could sleep for the night. After the old man had left, Tony looked at Jess. *"Si, Amigo, he is indeed a salty old man, as you say. He said that two men entered the barn last night but they were surprised to find themselves staring into the Winchester. He got off two rounds as they ran out the door but he wasn't sure if he hit them or not."*

Jess begin to laugh. "You don't say! I'll bet they were the thieves that stole Breathtaker. Emanuel said they would not stay in jail for very long if they could come up with a few pesos. I sure believe that to be true now, because the fat policeman sure took the money that Emanuel had taken off one of them when we had the fight. They are not likely to come back tonight if they ran into trouble here last night. The old man's Winchester probably made believers out of them."

"Amigo let me have one of the weapons. I am a fair marksman and I, like my son am not afraid to use it if it is necessary."

Jess pulled the .38 Smith & Wesson out from under his shirt and handed it to Tony. The lantern the old rancher left hanging by the door cast an amber glow in the barn. The two men talked as they rolled out their bedrolls.

Chapter 18

The door to the barn squeaked and slowly opened in the cool gray dawn, as the glow from the rancher's lantern cast light into the barn. Suddenly, awakened from a deep, peaceful sleep, both Jess and Tony sat up. The man had a full pot of boiling coffee and three tin cups. He sat down on a bale of hay and poured coffee into the cups and handed a cup to each of them. "I told you he was a good man, Tony. That's service in bed, I'd say."

"*Si, Amigo, he is a very good man.*"

Tony thanked the man and as they drank the hot coffee, Tony told him that he was Emanuel's father and expressed his appreciation for the help he gave Jess by providing him with what he needed so that he could catch the killer. The rancher began to talk freely and the two of them talked for a long time. They talked as though they had known each other for many years. Jess poured each of them another cup of coffee and sat listening to them speak in Spanish as they continued their conversation.

The rancher stood up then walked over to the feed room and shoveled a gallon of oats into a bucket. He carried them over to Breathtaker and as he entered the stall he rubbed Breathtaker on the shoulder then began to speak to him in Spanish. Jess hoped that Breathtaker understood what the man was saying because he sure didn't. The rancher petted Breathtaker for a little while and then poured the bucket of oat into the trough.

Jess looked over at Tony. "What did he say to

Breathtaker?"

"He said that Breathtaker was the prettiest horse that he has ever seen and that he sure would like to have a colt out of him and his best Spanish mare. He said that if he had such a colt he would win all the money in Mexico when the colt was old enough to race," said Tony.

Jess reached in his pocket and pulled out two twenty dollar bills and handed them to the man. He had done a great job caring for Breathtaker and he had probably kept the two men from stealing him again. The rancher smiled and tucked the twenty dollar bills deep into his pocket and politely tipped his hat.

"Gracias, Señor," he said.

After Breathtaker had finished eating, Jess took the halter and lead rope hanging by the door and walked over to Breathtaker's stall and stepped inside. Breathtaker stretched his long, sleek neck out and smelled the halter. Jess slipped it over his nose and buckled it over the head.

"Now you can go home big boy," said Jess, as he petted the colt on the neck. Jess led Breathtaker out of the barn then loaded him into the trailer. Jess turned to Tony. "Tell him he can have the small racing saddle and blanket. They belonged to the thieves that stole him," said Jess.

"Mucho gracias, Señor," said the old man as he lifted the finder of the small saddle and began examining it.

Jess shook the old man's tan, weathered hand, smiled and looked the old man straight in the eyes. "Tell him goodbye for me Tony." Tony told the old man goodbye and the two men loaded into the Ford and drove away for Juarez. Breathtaker stood in the slant stall of the trailer quietly but very alert as the trailer rattled down the drive. He was on his way to Oklahoma and home at last.

Chapter 19

The morning sun was just peeking over the horizon, casting its glow on the distant mountain range to the northwest. Jess remembered that was the direction and place where he and Breathtaker had finally caught up with the killer. This was some rough country, he thought. It was a country where a man could ride a horse two full days in the direction of the mountains and still be miles away from them. The week that Jess had spent in Mexico seemed as though it had been six months. He longed to return to Oklahoma and back to normal life once again. He followed Tony's direction to his house then pulled in the circle drive and stopped.

"Amigo, after you deliver the horses and get them headed back home, bring your wife here and we will be waiting to meet her."

"It will likely be a couple of hours before we return. I will have to tell the entire story to Alex before he leaves."

Jess pulled out of the drive and headed for the border check point. As they drove up to the check station, the Border patrol officer stepped up to the window and asked all the usual questions. He asked if Jess was a U.S citizen, about what was in the truck, and if there were goods in excess of certain quantities and dollar value. He then asked for health papers for crossing with the horses. Jess handed him the paperwork and he examined them carefully.

"Mr. Steel, everything seems to be in order. Have a

nice trip," said the Border Patrol officer as he motioned him on. Suddenly Jess's blood ran cold and a weakness filled his body. He was still in possession of the .25 automatic. He had clearly forgotten about it being in his boot. He had meant to give it to Tony while at the house. Jess rolled the truck window down and took a deep breath of cool, fresh air. "Boy! I was lucky that time!"

Jess turned onto highway 54 and headed north. He had seen the sign coming in that gave direction to the airport and knew that it was only a matter of minutes before he would arrive. As he rode along airport road, he could see the airport straight ahead. He turned into the long-term parking lot and waited for Susan and Alex to arrive. It was only a matter of minutes before they came in the gate. Alex had already seen the truck and trailer before coming in the gate and drove straight to where Jess was parked. Susan slid from the seat of the pick-up and ran to Jess and hugged him and began to cry. "I've been worried that you would never get back," she said, as Jess held her tightly.

"It was some ordeal and I'm just happy to get Breathtaker back and thankful to get out of there alive." They stood and talked for a little while and then Alex couldn't hold it any longer.

"What happened down there Jess?"

"Well, I'll tell you what, let's get the trailer hooked to your truck and then we'll get out of here and go to a truck stop and get some coffee and I'll tell you all about it."

Alex opened the door to the three-horse slant and then stepped inside with Breathtaker. He slid his hand along the colts back until he got to the neck and then he placed an arm around the colt's slick, gray neck and began to talk to him. "I've missed you, big boy, around that barn and if I ever get you back, they'll pay hell stealing you again. I bought a big Doberman yesterday from a man that said he was a good watch dog and I plan for him to be your stable mate, so don't you go too hard on that dog, you hear me." Alex took the lead rope and backed the colt out of the trailer to let him walk around a few minutes. Breathtaker stood proud, looking all around with his head high.

Susan stood still clutching Jess's hand, "You are a picture just waiting to be painted and we're glad to have you back, Breathtaker." She said.

Alex loaded Breathtaker back into the trailer and they hurriedly pulled out of the parking lot and headed for the truck stop on highway 54 to get coffee. After they had gone into the restaurant and sat at a table, Jess ordered coffee for everyone.

Susan was first to speak. "Jess, I was at the bank yesterday and John told me that you had made a large deposit. He said it came from Mexico. What in the devil is going on? John couldn't understand it, and I sure couldn't either."

Jess smiled, "Well, Breathtaker and I won us a horse race out there in the desert and that deposit was the purse," said Jess, as he continued to smile.

Alex cast a quick eye at Jess, "That must have been a stakes race of some kind. Jess, Susan said it was about $25,000.00."

Jess pushed his coffee away and sat back. "It was a stakes race all right. My life was at stake. That money was the reward Breathtaker got for catching a thief and a killer out in the middle of a Mexican desert. Alex, you should have seen it. I was riding Breathtaker early that morning and it was just after daylight and we were on the trail of the killer. I spotted him up ahead and we got to within fifty yards of him before he looked back and saw us coming. I sat down tight, got me a firm hand full of mane and screamed just like you did the day he ran out from under you when you were trying to teach him how to break out of the gate. That Mexican had a fifty yard head start but Breathtaker pinned his ears flat on his head and he made one hell of a run. I started talking to him as we began to close ground, and he just got faster. I didn't know a horse could run that fast, Alex. We caught him right out in the middle of the desert and he was riding as hard as his horse could carry him. Alex, Breathtaker is one fine horse and we will breed every mare we've got to him next year."

"I knew it! I knew he had a hand in catching that killer. I would have bet on it. After Susan told me that you had caught the man that killed your friend, I knew it."

Jess took about thirty minutes and told the entire story with out stopping. Alex and Susan listened intently as Jess described as best he could the chain of events.

"I guess the only fun that I had was catching that killer and getting to ride the best horse that I've ever sat my bottom on," said Jess.

Alex shifted his hat and smiled. "Man, that's about as near to a John Wayne movie as I have ever heard. What I would have given to see you catch that Killer. Man, oh man."

"Drink up. We don't want the horse to over heat in the trailer. You need to get him rolling toward home, Alex. Breathtaker has had it kind of rough since he was stolen so just give him plenty of cool water, a big paddock with grass, and let him just be a horse for a while. He's earned it."

Chapter 20

After Alex had gone, Susan and Jess rode back across the border. This time he wasn't carrying the .25 automatic. He had given it to Alex before he left. Susan seemed to be a little uneasy and suddenly asked if they would be safe at Tony's house.

"Sure. Tony is a powerful man and apparently a very rich one. He owns two or three large markets here in Juarez and is widely known. Susan, you just can't imagine how much help Tony has been down here."

"You're not going to keep the reward money, are you, Jess?" she asked.

"Well, I have already tried to get him to accept our check for the reward and I've told him I did not feel right accepting such a large sum for something I would have done for anyone. He flatly refuses to accept our check and he apparently is so set on it that he finally told me that the reward was Breathtaker's."

Susan sat looking out the window of the truck as they rode on. "Well, if he won't accept it, what else can we do?"

"Nothing."

"The funeral is tomorrow at ten o'clock and I want us to buy a large flower arrangement for the family. You know, carnations or something really nice," said Jess.

"Jess, we don't know where to order flowers down here. Is there someone, perhaps a member of the family who can help us with that?"

"When we get to Tony's house and I get a chance, I

will talk to Emanuel's mother-in-law. She is a very nice lady and she will likely be able to assist." As they turned into the driveway, Susan was all eyes. "My goodness, this is a very nice place," she said, as the truck rolled to a stop.

As they walked through the stone walled courtyard Susan noticed that it was landscaped with many desert plants. A large, double wrought-iron gate lay open and beyond it an elm tree grew up in the center of the courtyard. The roof of the courtyard had been built around the tree and it was beautiful. A meandering, cobble-stone sidewalk led up to the front door. Jess rang the door bell. The door opened and it was Tony who answered the door.

"Welcome to my casa, Mr. and Mrs. Steel," he said politely.

"Tony, I would like you to meet the boss around our house. This is Susan. Susan, this is Tony."

"Señora, I am pleased to have the opportunity to meet the wife of such a good man as yours. He is special and will always be special in this family. I could never tell you how much this man has done to help this family," he said. *"I assume you have luggage that needs to be unloaded, no?"*

He no sooner got the words out of his mouth than two young men rushed out to the truck and brought Susan's luggage into the house.

"Your house is beautiful, Tony. It is so large and spacious. I love the many arches and heavy timbers. It is perfect in every way," said Susan as she scanned her surroundings.

"Gracias, Señora, but there is one thing that will create a large vacancy in this casa. The lack of my son," he said.

"You have our deepest symphony, Tony. I have never lost a son, but I know it must be a terrible loss," said Susan.

"Come, let me introduce you to the other members

of the family," said Tony.

As they walked down the wide, long foyer into the family room Jess could see that Susan was very impressed with the house.

"Everyone come into the family room, I want you to meet the wonderful wife of our hero. This is Senora Susan Steel, from Oklahoma. Please make her welcome. She is a very special guest in my casa. We should have a very special meal for her." he said.

Jess could tell by looking at Susan that she was a little embarrassed by so much attention. Jess looked at her and smiled and squeezed her hand gently.

"Tony, you're right. She is truly special to me," said Jess.

Tony let out a laugh then turned to Susan smiling. *"Tomorrow, Señora, in the evening we will go to my market and you can shop for whatever you may like. I have a wide selection of goods from which you may choose. You pick what you like and I will package them and ship the goods to your casa in Oklahoma,"* said Tony.

"Come let me show you the casa," stated Elena, one of the young women who had been introduced as Tony's niece. She took Susan's hand and led her up the stairs to a large, rustic balcony that overlooked the family room, and then she began showing her some of the many pieces of primitive, hand-carved furniture that decorated the beautiful house.

Tony and Jess walked to the study and sat down. Tony poured them a small glass of tequila and began asking about horses.

"I have a small one hundred and twenty acre farm to the east of the city located in the Rio Grande valley that grows very good grass. I am so impressed with your Breathtaker that I have decided to purchase a few good horses with which to start a herd."

Jess quickly sat forward in his chair. "How would

you like to have a son of Breathtaker for a herd stallion?"

"I would like that very much. What would a young horse like that cost?"

"Since you will not take the reward money back, I will give you an offspring of my horse and that is final and non-negotiable."

"Amigo, you are a hard man, but a good man and I will take your offer with pleasure. I also will purchase some mares from you if you have them to sell or if you do not I will employ you to find and purchase such for me. That too, Amigo, is final, and is also non- negotiable. Now, Amigo, what will five good mares cost?"

"Well, I will have to look around and see what I can find and what I have that would cross well with Breathtaker. I will have the mares by next spring and will breed them all to Breathtaker so that you will have a crop of foals the first year. You can expect to pay $ 5,000.00 to $8,000.00 each for good brood mares. Of course you can pay much more, but I do not see why you should. I believe that I can find the right kind of mares and mares that you will like for that kind of money."

"Then it is done. You find the mares and I will transfer the money to your bank with which to purchase them."

"Tony, Breathtaker is not a proven sire yet, but in time, you could possibly have the finest herd of horses in Mexico. I am looking for Breathtaker to become an important sire someday. Many of his get could be runners like him, you know."

"I know that is a very good possibility, Amigo. The old man that loaned you the horse with which to help catch the killer, we talked of this very thing and he believes Breathtaker will be a great horse. I also know that I shall give the old rancher one of the offspring. He is a good old man and wished for a horse such as Breathtaker. He is deserving of such an animal and he shall have it."

Chapter 21

It was Sunday and the funeral service was a sad and a very emotional ceremony. It was obvious the funeral home was likely the best one in Mexico for the service was very well conducted. There was a mountain of flowers and the large arrangement of carnations that Jess and Susan had made arrangements for was beautiful and well displayed along with dozens of others displaying vivid colors and design. It wasn't a long funeral service as Jess would have guessed it would be. The service only lasted about forty-five minutes. After the service was over at the Mission, a long and very slow procession to the cemetery was led by the City Police Department, where Emanuel had worked. The body was carried by carriage pulled by six beautiful matching bay horses wearing sterling silver trimmed harness and then there were thirty mounted policemen on palominos. There were hundreds of policemen from all over northern Mexico who marched behind a band that played Spanish hymns. The sounds of the Mexican trumpeters were soothing to the ear and the sounds made by the trumpets echoed through the streets as they made their way toward the cemetery where Emanuel would be laid to rest. Jess suddenly realized what a powerful man Tony Gonzalez was in Juarez, Mexico, for there were thousands of people gathered on the streets to pay their respects to his family.

The house was relatively quiet after the funeral with

only the immediate family there. It was obvious that Jess and Susan's presence seemed to help the family to forget their grief temporarily.

Jess and Susan were sitting in the large family room when Tony entered. *"It is now time to go to the market, Señora Steel. Come, I will go with you as will some of the women. I know that Elena will go, for she is a great shopper. There is much to see and we should start immediately."*

"We can wait until tomorrow, Tony," said Susan.

"Señora, it is good that we go now. It is the way that Emanuel would have wanted it to be. Come. We go now." Tony picked up his straw hat and headed for the door and they were off to the market.

The evening was filled with Susan and Elena looking at everything in the markets but purchasing little. Susan bought a set of Mexican bowls that displayed colorful floral decoration, along with a set of place mats for decoration. She found various colorful woven blankets and pieces of pottery that she liked and as the day came to an end, the goods were wrapped and carefully packed. A young Mexican man assured Susan that her things would be shipped the following day to the ranch in Oklahoma.

As Jess and Susan walked out of the market toward the truck, Jess turned to Tony. "Amigo, we must now go home. I have a lot of work to do and too, I want to begin immediately selecting and putting together your group of brood mares," said Jess as he reached out and shook Tony's hand.

"I am saddened that you leave, Amigo, but I know you must go back to your home. I only ask that you and your beautiful wife come back and visit me at least once each year, for I know that I will have many little Breathtakers for you to see. Please take good care of the wonderful stallion for he is my life long friend as are you. Vaya con Dios, Amigo."

Jess and Susan quickly crossed the border and took Interstate 10 west out of El Paso toward Las Cruces.

"Where are we going now?" asked Susan.

"Well, I don't guess we are in too big of a hurry and I thought we would make a loop through New Mexico and just look around a bit. I read a tourist guide that I picked up at truck stop just outside of Roswell on my way down and it said that there was a very good place to eat Mexican food at Las Cruces. It's supposed to be one of the best in the country. The name of the place is 'La Posta.' It's in the old town of Mesilla and the building once served as the Butterfield stage stop. It's not very far over there, so I thought we'd just check it out. We'll spend the night there and then maybe ease on up to Santa Fe and look around a little before going home," said Jess.

Susan cast a teasing eye toward Jess. "Jess Steel, you are just full of surprises."

Jess smiled, winked at Susan and suddenly begun to laugh. "Well, Susan, didn't you hear what Tony said? He said that I was a good man and you don't need to forget that."

As they sped along highway 10 they crossed the Texas state line into New Mexico and off to the west lay the wide Rio Grande valley with its many alfalfa fields and large dairies. There with huge stacks of alfalfa that had been baled for the dairy cattle. There were hundreds of acres of pecan trees casting their shadows long in the late evening sun. Just across the road to the east the landscape was completely different. There was a gentle rolling desert dotted with Spanish bayonet and various species of cacti and sage. It had rained recently and the shallow roots of the desert sage had glutted the water and were in full bloom, creating a cascade of purple haze that stretched to the picturesque Organ Mountains with their tall irregular peaks. It was a beautiful part of the country and Jess knew that it was filled with colorful history of the early west. Most of the new Mexicans who live here now were descendants of people who had been here before New Mexico had become a state. There had been battles for title of this land and there had been many raids conducted by the Apaches on the town. Many desperadoes passed through along the Camino trail and some even lived in the area. Many of the desperate men who had passed through were chased through this country trying to make it across the border into Mexico and away from the long arm of the law. As they rode on, Jess pointed toward the mountains.

"Susan, look at that! Look at the sun shining on the mountains."

The late evening sun was beginning to set behind a purple thunderhead to the west and rays of light cast pastel beams against the jagged peaks as though attaching themselves to the mountains or perhaps pointing to the natural beauty of the landscape.

As they entered the outskirts of Las Cruses, the exit sign on highway 10 read: *Avenida de Mesilla* one mile. Jess turned on the right directional signal and steered the truck onto the off ramp and slowed. At the bottom of the ramp he stopped. Not knowing where he was going, he turned left toward the Rio Grande River. They hadn't gone more than a quarter of a mile and to their left there was the Siesta R.V. park with its neat stucco southwest-style office sporting the red tile roof covering a lean-to porch. To the right sitting off the road a way was a development of beautiful southwest style houses casting shadows long in the late evening. A long stucco and rock fence separated the houses from the commercial property along the avenue and there was a pottery sales place and various other businesses along the drive. A little farther on there was another sign and it was the sign they were hoping to find and had blindly stumbled upon. It was a historical sign that read: 'Historic Old Mesilla, one-fourth mile.' Jess turned the truck north and followed the signs onto a narrow street that had at some time in the distant past been designed for horse and buggy. The street led into the old town of Mesilla. There was a plaza that lay in the center of the town, lit with old cast iron pole lamps. At one end of the plaza there was a historical marker that revealed the significance of the old town and at the other end there stood a stately, ornate cathedral. There were park benches scattered about for the many visitors and surrounding the plaza were many shops and stores, many with fronts still intact as they were in the 1800s or before. On one of the store fronts there were bullet holes near the top of the door, showing evidence of a shoot-out sometime in the distant past. On one street corner stood the original territorial capital of Arizona Territory that had been converted into a unique store and the place where Billy the Kid had been tried and sentenced to hang.

As they walked into the La Posta restaurant it was like stepping back in time two hundred years. It was all there, much of it just as it had been when it was the Butterfield stage stop, everything, that is, except the strong people, of that era. People were there and they were good people too, but they were of a softer kind, a more civilized kind. Then Jess suddenly wondered if that was all good. As he looked around he saw a young man come in wearing a clean western hat and nice lizard-skin boots and he wondered how that brand of modern-day cowboy would have made out in those mountains a few days ago when he and Emanuel had been ambushed.

After they had finished eating, Jess paid the bill and they walked out of the restaurant onto the street and they strolled all the way around the plaza window shopping. It was a unique place and Susan fell in love with many shops and southwestern displays in the windows.

A gentle, warm evening breeze stirred through the old town and kicked up small dust along the curb. Jess suddenly realized that he was a lucky man. He was lucky all right, lucky in more ways than one. He had his horse back and he had managed to get out of that ordeal alive. Most of all, he was happy to be enjoying the company of Susan again.

Chapter 22

After having spent the past four days in New Mexico with Susan, enjoying their leisure travel while viewing the beautiful southwest landscape, the green country of eastern Oklahoma and the ranch seemed to Jess to have changed. It appeared to be greener, much greener than it had been before he left. Along the quarter-mile drive leading up to the barn the roses Susan had planted two years before were in full bloom, creating a floral delight of red, yellow and pink against the white pipe and cable fences. There had been an abundance of rain since he had departed and the pastures were lush. Jess noticed the brood mares grazing near the fence with their foals scampering and playing young horse games, whatever kind of horse games they play.

As Jess pulled up to the barn, he noticed that Alex had turned Breathtaker out into a paddock that covered about six acres to the south of the barn. Jess slid out of the truck seat and whistled at Breathtaker just as he had done when he was little and they were playing the hide and seek game. Breathtaker's head suddenly flew up then he bolted toward Jess at a dead run. He had fully rested now and was ready for a game or perhaps a sugar cube that he knew Jess always had for him. Jess watched him as he bore down on the fence where he was standing and wondered if he would be able to stop before wiping out him and the fence. Breathtaker skidded to a stop just short of hitting the fence and nickered at Jess.

Jess reached through the cable fence and began rubbing his soft coat. "Are you rested up big boy? How are you doing these days?" Jess thought about what a pleasure he had been to ride down south of the border. He also knew that he had plans for him and Breathtaker to examine some of the country on the back side of the ranch in a very few days. They would just look at the deer and maybe check a few fences that extend through the timber. Alex usually checked the back fences at least twice each year but he also knew that a dead tree or limb could have fallen on the fence and would need to be removed. Jess reached into his shirt pocket and pulled out a sugar cube and gave it to Breathtaker. Jess seldom went to the barn without a sugar cube or two. Breathtaker smacked and chomped the sugar cube as he tossed his head back and forth, savoring the sweetness. Jess stood watching Breathtaker for a minute and then he spied Alex coming out of the barn toward him.

"Hi Jess! Welcome back," said Alex, smiling and showing at least half of his teeth through the graying mustache as he approached, "Jess, I've entered him in a $ 5,000.00 allowance race to be run next week. He's got the field outclassed by a country mile. Figured we would let Breathtaker pick up a little easy feed money. The best part of all is; they have written a
$25,000.00 stakes race for two-year-old colts and winners of two races. If we can pick up the race next week we'll be qualified for the stakes race. We'll give it a try if you agree. That stakes race will likely attract some pretty good horseflesh, if I'm guessing right," said Alex, as he cast a questioning look at Jess.

"Alex, he's been out of training for over a month now. Do you think he's up to it?"

Alex looked at Jess and then wasted a little Beach Nut tobacco juice. "Jess, you've rode him over half of Mexico, then run down and caught that thief down there a few days ago. Seems to me, he aught to be able to win a little ole three-hundred-fifty yard race, don't you think?"

Jess slapped Breathtaker on the shoulder and then looked at Alex and smiled.

"Hell, yes, he's ready."

Alex went into the tack room and picked up Breathtaker's halter and brought him in and put him in his stall. It was getting late and it was feeding time, so he gave Breathtaker his grain and an extra feeding of alfalfa.

"Sorry to have to put you up in your stall but we've got a little track work to do the next four or five days, big boy," said Alex, as he ran his hand down Breathtaker's side. Then stepped out of the stall.

"Don't plan on getting him started too soon, Alex, He and I have a trip planned in the morning. I want to ride him out to check the back fences before he becomes a race horse again."

"Well, I'll be damn! He charmed you, didn't he Jess? He's got a way of doing that all right. That big gray devil is a pleasure to ride."

The next morning, Jess got to the barn early and gave Breathtaker his ration of grain. Gray light was just moving in when Jess mounted and rode Breathtaker away from the barn. A light fog hung low across the pasture and to the south and down near a patch of timber, three white-tail deer fed cautiously on tender shoots of bluestem, lifting their heads frequently to watch the horse and rider until they moved out of sight. Breathtaker was fresh and pranced sassily for a little while before settling down into a comfortable, quick walk. A rabbit nibbling on small vegetation hopped out of the trail and into the brush and an owl flew from the top of a dead tree where he had been stately poised to eye field mice in the night. They rode on for a while until they entered the timber. There was a big stand of red oak trees in the creek bottom and Jess reined up as soon as they were well into the timber. A gray squirrel with her young ones scampered through the trees, jumping from limb to limb as they busily fed on ripe acorns. It was quiet in the woods and the only sounds that Jess could hear were the birds coming off their roosts and the squeak of the saddle leather. Jess put his hand to his mouth and gave the call of an owl and suddenly a wild turkey gobbler answered the sound from somewhere far down the creek. It was a peaceful morning and there was no hurry to move on so they stood and watched the squirrels for a while. Jess remembered when he was a boy growing up down in Arkansas and the many times he had gone hunting at that hour. It was his favorite time of day and as he sat on his horse he suddenly knew that life was good. Then he thought about the two Mexicans he had killed down south of the border and for a moment wondered if he really had to do that, even though he knew that they would have killed both him and Emanuel just as soon as they could get them in their sights. That was what they were doing. They were waiting to kill them at ambush. Even though, Jess knew it could not have been avoided, it bothered him some that he had actually taken the life of another man.

Breathtaker pranced lightly and Jess knew he was anxious to go so he nudged the colt with his right heel and rode on slowly through the trees and down the creek bottom. Suddenly Breathtaker's head came up and his ears pricked forward as a deer lunged from its bed directly ahead of them and dashed into the brush flipping the white flag of its tail with every bounce.

"Easy boy, it's just a deer," said Jess, as Breathtaker snorted and quickly shied to the left trying to turn back. Jess knew there was something about a fleeing deer that always seemed to stir up a horse and Breathtaker was no exception. He was fully stirred up right about then. Jess petted the colt on the neck and continued to talk to him until he settled down, as they rode on down the creek. After they had ridden for a while Jess pulled up and dismounted and lit up a cigarette. There was a dead log nearby that had fallen sometime in the distant past so Jess sat down on the log. He needed to think, he needed to get the killing sorted out in his mind and put it behind him. He pulled his hat off and hung it on a small branch nearby and pushed back his dark hair, letting the hair flow through his fingers. Suddenly he dodged a little from the tenderness of his still sore head. He swore lightly. "Damn, I guess that's the answer. Hell's fire, one of those Mexicans came really close to killing me. I absolutely had no choice in the matter. It was either me or them. Now that's it in a nutshell, "thought Jess. Jess crushed the cigarette out with his boot, assuring that it was completely out, and then mounted up and rode on. The early sun was still casting long shadows, showing its early morning glow through the timber over his left shoulder. Jess knew that he must turn a little to his left in order to intersect the back section line and the fence that he planned to check. Breathtaker was a constant movement of curiosity and looked at everything in his line of sight as they moved on south. Jess could feel Breathtaker's muscles working underneath the saddle and the fluid movement of his quick walk and as the saddle leather squeaked, they moved on. Suddenly Breathtaker's ears perked up and Jess quickly glanced in the direction the colt was looking. A big bobcat hunkered on a low hanging limb of a big oak looking at the approaching horse and rider and then gracefully sprang to the ground and sneaked off into the brush. Jess knew that the bobcat wasn't waiting to pounce on them but was likely waiting in ambush for a deer to make a deadly mistake and walk under the tree.

As they came upon the back fence, Jess swung to the west and rode along, looking for suspect fallen trees or limbs that could have possibly fallen on the fence but found none. It was an enjoyable ride and as they continued they came upon numerous small, open meadows covered with wild yellow and gold flowers. Now and again Jess saw wild honeysuckle growing on the fence and could smell the wonderful fragrance. They saw more deer along the way and Breathtaker seemed to be getting used to them now, not shying so much.

It was mid-morning when Jess and Breathtaker reached the back southwest corner of the ranch and Jess pulled up and dismounted. He tied Breathtaker to a small bush and gathered some dried limbs and built a small fire for coffee. He filled the small pot with water form the canteen and added a half handful of coffee that he had taken out of Susan's coffee canister early that morning.

"I bet you're about ready for a drink of water," said Jess, as he talked to Breathtaker. The big, gray colt rubbed his head on the trunk of the small tree he was tied too, scratching where the bridle lay behind his ears.

"We'll be at the creek in a half hour or so and then you can drink your fill, big boy," said Jess.

The coffee was good and Jess sat down and leaned back against a tree and enjoyed the peaceful sounds of the woods and thought about the up-coming race that Alex had Breathtaker entered in. Jess tossed the last of the coffee on the fire and scraped dirt over the steaming coals with his boot. Then mounted up again.

As they came upon the creek Jess could hear the water as it trickled across rocks and gurgled as it flowed around exposed roots of a tree that grew down near the water. The trail crossing the creek was a mass of deer tracks. It was their favorite crossing place and the trail was well used. The wind had come up and a faint breeze stirred the trees now. The leaves above whispered to the wooded stillness of mid-morning as Breathtaker drank long and deep from the cold, clear creek water.

After Breathtaker finished drinking, Jess mounted up and rode on north along the fence for a mile and then turned northeast angling across the big pasture toward the barn. Breathtaker stepped lightly now and Jess could feel the mounting spring in the gray colt's walk. Breathtaker was thinking about the grain he knew he would get when they got there because it was feeding time and he knew it.

Chapter 23

Jess and Susan were standing out at the rail when the starting gates flew open and ten lunging horses headed for the wire.

"They're off!" The announcer voice shouted over the field. *"It's number one, Breathtaker by a nose on the inside as they break from a good start. Now it's Whirlaway and Breathtaker battling for the lead. Its number six on the outside making his bid. Breathtaker is now taking the lead; he's headed to the wire folks!!! It's Breathtaker in front by one! No! Two full lengths now!"*

They were half way down the stretch now and heading for the wire when the small Jockey slapped Breathtaker on the shoulder and begin to talk to him just as Alex had directed. "Come on. Come on colt, show them how it's done," shouted the jockey over the sound of the forty pounding hoofs.. Breathtaker's ears were pinned flat against his head when he hit high gear and swept the last one hundred yards to the finish wire.

"Oh My!! My!! My, my folks!! It's Breathtaker by seven lengths and a possible new track record," shouted the caller.

"Is he a race horse or is he a race horse?" shouted Jess, clutching Susan's hand and heading to the winners circle. Breathtaker pranced nervously as he got his picture taken. He was still ready to run. Jess rubbed Breathtaker's sleek neck then reached in his shirt pocket and pulled out the sugar cube. The jockey sprang down after the picture and as they left the winners circle, the jockey looked straight into Jess's eyes.

"I've rode lots of good horses, Jess, but this colt is by far the best I've ever sat down on. I believe he could win the 'All American Derby' by daylight," said the jockey. Alex Haygood knew what winning the prestigious, one million dollar 'All American' could mean to all of them. He'd been there before and he was riding the winner when they crossed the finish line. Alex glanced at Jess and smiled. Then he led Breathtaker toward the test barn.

The day after the race, Jess sat quietly just outside the tack room, smoking a cigarette and reading his favorite racing magazine. Alex pulled up a lawn chair and sat for a minute.

"What do you think, Jess?"

"Think about what?"

"Breathtaker and the All American."

Jess laid the magazine down and thought for a minute. "Well, I pretty much had my mind made up to retire him and not run him anymore when I left Mexico."

"I was afraid of that," said Alex with a depressed look on his face.

"Susan thinks we should run him. I don't know. I've made some commitments to breed a few mares to him for Tony and I'd have to call him and make other arrangements. I'm just not convinced that we really have a shot at winning. I know he's good, but is he really *that* good? Alex, let's wait until after the stakes race you've entered him in week after next, then we'll talk about it some more."

Alex looked at Jess and chuckled. "Jess, if winning that race is what it will take to convince you that Breathtaker is the best in the country, you may as well get Susan and go on down there and sit down by the winners circle. He'll win it by daylight."

"Alex, you have my word, if we get an impressive win. Well, I'll have to go see the banker to get him paid up in the futurity, but we'll do it if he is that good."

"Yi-Hoo! Clear the road boys. We're coming to New Mexico!" shouted Alex. You could have heard him for a country mile. He was about as excited as a little man can get.

The next ten days were busy with training and getting ready for the upcoming race at Blue Ribbon Downs. Breathtaker went to the track every morning for light work; he got his bath, rested and spent the rest of his time nibbling on alfalfa hay for the balance of the day. The last two days before the race, Alex didn't work Breathtaker. He spent a lot of time grooming him and talking to him. He didn't want him to work off any energy. He wanted him ready to turn on the afterburner. After all, there were some really good horses in the race and all of them were "AAA" horses. Alex knew that Breathtaker would have to put forth some effort to beat them impressively and Jess was looking for an impressive win or the All American would be off.

It was Saturday morning and a light southerly breeze fluttered the flag above Blue Ribbon downs as Jess drove the ford pulling the horse trailer down the drive to the haul in barn. It was the day of the big $25,000.00 stakes race and the field would be full. There would be ten speedsters running for the purse and they would all be ready. Jess stopped the truck and walked to the back of the trailer and opened the gate. He stepped inside and took hold of Breathtaker's halter and backed him out of the trailer. Breathtaker stood quietly with his head high looking at four other horses hooked to a walker at the barn next door.

"You better get your mind on business, big boy, we come to race, not play with the girls," said Alex.

Breathtaker followed Alex into the barn and stepped into the freshly-bedded stall and immediately checked the feed trough just in case there was some feed to be had. Jess went to the truck and brought all of the items he needed to get Breathtaker ready for the up-coming race. There were the leg wraps to be applied and there was last-minute grooming to be done but Alex knew that he would be ready by post time. Alex also knew that he would stay with Breathtaker and be with him every minute prior to the race. There would be no way that Alex would trust anyone to horse-sit for him especially after the trauma of his being stolen prior to the Black Gold finals. That just wasn't going to happen.

It was twenty minutes until two when Jess led Breathtaker into the saddling paddock. It was the eighth race and Breathtaker was the last horse to arrive. Alex led him into the number one stall. They had been lucky with the position draw and had drawn the 'one hole,' or one position next to the rail. Jess placed the small saddle pad and saddle on Breathtaker's back and pulled the girth tight and then did a general check to make sure that everything was correct. As usual Breathtaker stood calmly. Many of the other speedsters reared and chomped their D-ring bits working themselves into a sweat. One of the horses reared and pawed the air almost striking his trainer, in a state of pre-race nervousness.

Jess heard the trumpeter start the familiar boots and saddles and the jockeys were boosted up on the ten speedsters.

"Just sit down, take a deep seat and ride. Slap him on the neck and call on him at two hundred yards and he'll go to work for you, then just ride him to the wire," said Alex, as he gave last minute instruction to the jockey.

As usual, Jess and Susan stood at the rail so they could get a close-up look at Breathtaker and the competition as they paraded by. Breathtaker pranced along with his head held high, his tail flowing in the breeze. The red silks the jockey wore matched the red blinkers and framed his sleek gray coat.

"Jess, he's the most beautiful horse I've ever seen," stated Susan quietly.

"He is a looker all right and someday, Susan, I want you to ride him. When you feel him moving under the saddle you know you're on a real horse and you're not apt to forget. He's as fine, as fine as horse flesh can get."

They watched as the horses rounded the track and made their way to the starting gates. Jess could feel the tightening in his stomach as pre-race nervousness began to set in. He knew Breathtaker would and could run well but there was always that doubt. Too many things can happen in a quarter horse race. There is seldom enough time for a horse to recover after the slightest mistake. They were all in the gates now, all but two and they were giving trouble behind the gates. Breathtaker stood quietly and seemingly ready to take care of the business at hand. The jockey sat down firmly and gathered up a hand full of Breathtaker's mane anticipating the fierce lunge that he knew was sure to come. He had ridden him before in the trials and knew that he would break hard when the gate flew open. The two speedsters at the outside stepped into the gates finally and a dead silence fell upon the area.

"*They're off,*" came the caller's voice as the ten exploding horses lunged hard out of the gate headed toward the finish line. Breathtaker was holding tight against the rail but the number two and three horses had him boxed in. No running room. No place to go. Suddenly the jockey saw a little space to his right and then pulled him in behind the number three horse and to the outside of the two front runners. Jess could see that Breathtaker was running well but he was a full length behind the two sprinting leaders. Then through the binoculars, he saw the little jockey reach out and slap Breathtaker on the neck and knew that he was talking to him, calling for more. They were half-way down the stretch now and there was very little time for

Breathtaker to recover. Suddenly the caller's voice changed pitch and rang out clearly over the roar of the crowd.

"Oh my, folks! It's Breathtaker making up ground fast on the outside. It's A-lot-o-cash in the lead and Heza Rebel Jet running second. Breathtaker now taking the lead, he's out front folks by a length and A-Lot-o-cash trying to hold on. Breathtaker now by two as Rebel Jet falls back into third position." Jess and Susan were waving the racing forms and screaming at the top of their lungs for their colt, and then the announcers call came clearly.

"It's Breathtaker the winner by four lengths, A-Lot-O-Cash second and Heza Rebel Jet comes in third," the caller shouted, as they swept under the wire. Jess clutched Susan around the waist with his right arm, picked her completely up and swirled her around.

"Winner's circle time! Come on Susan, we've got to have a picture of this one." When they got to the winner circle, Alex had made a mad dash on the pony horse from the starting gates and stood smiling, totally overwhelmed with excitement.

"I knew it Jess, I knew it, and there was no doubt in my mind that he was the best. Look out, Ruidoso Downs, here we come! Ye-Hoo!" shouted Alex.

Jess rubbed Breathtaker's neck with his left hand, reached in his shirt pocket with his right, and pulled out the sugar cube then gave it to Breathtaker.

Chapter 24

The next few days after the race were filled with hard work for both Alex and Jess making plans and getting ready for the richest and most prestigious quarter horse race in the world. Jess had paid Breathtaker up in the futurity and Susan had been working out the lodging arrangements. Alex had made arrangements with Mike Tapp to take care of things while they were away and he had already started coming over to the barn, getting familiar with the feeding routine. Alex had been working Breathtaker daily, getting him in top form before going to Ruidoso for the trials.

It was two weeks before the trials and Jess had helped Alex with his evening chores at the barn. After they finished, they stood in front of Breathtaker's stall talking.

Jess stood silent for a minute. "Alex, if you don't have anything planned, Susan has made a big pot of chicken and dumplings. She told me to ask you up to the house for dinner, if you don't have anything to do. I thought we might do a little planning for the big race."

"I see no reason why not. I've had those chicken and dumplings before that Susan fixes and I'm not about to miss an opportunity like that. Let's go, I'm starving."

Susan was delighted that Alex had accepted her invitation for dinner. "Hi, guys, just in time. It's not much but maybe we'll have enough," said Susan, as she set the last of the food on the table. Jess knew she was being modest. Susan knew well how to set a table and she was one fine cook, too.

After they had finished eating, Jess poured each of them a cup of coffee. "I have thought about it all day. What do you all think about pulling out for New Mexico a few days early?"

Alex set his coffee down. "That's the best news I've heard. There is a difference in elevation out there in the high country and that would give Breathtaker time to adjust to the thinner air, and I would have a chance to work him at the track a few times before the trials."

"What can I do to help you get everything we need from the barn packed?"

Alex smiled. "Nothing. I've had everything packed since before the last race. There never was a doubt in my mind that we were going. All we've got to do is wrap Breathtaker's legs and load him in the trailer."

"What about you, Susan? Are you ready?"

"I'm all packed. I just need to call ahead and get the lodging reservations changed but that won't be a problem. I can do that tonight."

Alex looked at Susan. "Don't make any reservations for me. I'm not taking any chances this time. I've got a cot and air mattress already loaded in the tack room of the trailer. I'm sleeping in the barn with Breathtaker."

Jess considered what Alex had said for a moment and knew there was no changing the little man's mind. "Have you made arrangements for a jockey?"

Alex smiled. "I've got Jackie. He will be coming down for both the trials and the derby. He knows Breathtaker like a book. He's rode him in every race he's run. Jackie has never had a shot at the All American and he's ready and deserves a big win."

Jess looked at Alex. "I was hoping you were going to say that. He a fine jockey and he will do his very dead level best to win, that's for sure."

"What time you all want to leave out?"

"The earlier the better will suit me," said Alex.

"We'll meet you at the barn at feeding time, but you should call Mike and let him know we are pulling out early."

"Mike will be at the barn in the morning to feed. I've already made arrangements for him to be there. I figured we may want to pull out early and not knowing what day we would be leaving, I just wanted him to be there so we would be free to go."

Jess looked at each of them. "Well, it sounds like we're ready to go, so in the morning we'll just head out."

"Susan that was the best dinner I have had since the last time I was here. It was delicious," said Alex, as he got up from the table to leave.

Susan cleared the dishes off the table. "Jess, he's really excited about having an opportunity to run in the All American again, isn't he?"

"I don't think he has ever been more excited than he is now and I just hope luck is with us and Breathtaker gets out of the gate in good fashion in both the trials and the Derby. That's the only thing that concerns me. I know that if he gets out good, he'll do well."

"Does that mean *win* Jess?"

"That means win. Susan. He's the best I've ever seen."

After Susan finished up in the kitchen, she went to the computer and made the necessary lodging arrangements. As she came out of the study she turned to Jess. "I made arrangements for renting a car for us while we are out there. That will let me have transportation to shop or just look around while you and Alex are at the track. Alex can take the truck at night so that he won't be without transportation."

"That is an excellent idea," said Jess.

Jess and Susan sat down in the den and watched the

T.V. for a while before going to bed. Jess was looking at the T.V but his mind was on Breathtaker and the All American Derby. He knew this likely would be his only shot at winning the big one because, a man just doesn't get a horse the caliber of Breathtaker but maybe once in a lifetime, if he's lucky.

After Jess went to bed he was awake for a long time, thinking about just how lucky he really was. His mind rolled back to the canyon down in Mexico when he had almost been killed by the thief's bullet. He thought about how he had finally recovered Breathtaker and what a price Tony's family had had to pay in the ordeal. Yes, he was a lucky man indeed, lucky in more ways than one. Jess pulled Susan close and held her tight. Then he closed his eyes and fell into a peaceful sleep.

Chapter 25

It was 7:30 when they pulled out onto interstate 40 headed for New Mexico. They talked throughout the day about a variety of subjects but mostly about racing and horses. Jess and Alex took turns at driving. They traded places at stops for fuel or at times when they stopped to check on Breathtaker. The Ford diesel hummed along, pulling the three-horse slant loaded with Breathtaker and all the racing gear. Alex had loaded a few bales of alfalfa and sacks of grain into the trailer to hold them for a few days until they could get hay at Ruidoso.

The late June sun was casting long shadows when they turned at Roswell and headed toward Ruidoso. The traffic was light and they had made good time on the way and no one seemed to be very tired. As they came off a high slope into the Hondo valley, Jess commented on the drive. "This drive through these mountains has always been beautiful. I've come through here in the fall and the colored leaves on the trees are a spectacular sight to behold."

"They sure are, Jess. I rode horses down here in 79 and 80 and I got a chance to see the fall colors then. I liked it out here really well. This area has a lot of history, you know."

As they rode through the mountains, highway 70 meandered through the narrow valley. Jess pointed to a small settlement down below that lay along the creek. "Speaking of history, there is some history down there. That little settlement is where Billy the Kid and some others had a gun battle during the Lincoln County wars of the 1800's. This area through these mountains is also the home of the Mascalero Apache Indians. There was a lot of conflict out through these mountains during those days. It was some kind of rough country then. I think it would have been my kind of life back then. I've always said I was born a hundred and fifty years too late. Just think about it. There's been many an old cowboy rode through here on horseback. I imagine they rode along that creek down there where it wasn't so rocky and also there was water for both them and their horses."

Jess was driving and Alex sat looking out the truck window. "I believe this mountain range is called the Sacramento range and to the north they connect to the Jicarilla Mountains. Fort Stanton is only about forty or fifty miles northwest of here."

Jess thought about that for a few minutes. "Fort Stanton played a big roll in the early settlement of the area. It was established for the purpose of keeping the Apaches in line during that time."

"Jess, you think that 'Billy the Kid' was as bad as they claimed him to be?"

"Well I've always wondered about that myself but from what I've read and stories I've heard, he was a pretty tough character. He killed two deputy sheriffs in a jail break and I don't know how many other people. I think almost every town in New Mexico claim their state's most famous outlaw spent time in their area and he may have, but from what I can find out, he actually grew up and spent his youth at Silver City, a town just northwest of here. I've heard stories that he would be seen in, say, the town of Mesilla down south then three or four days later be seen in Santa Fe. That may or may not be true. Santa Fe is three or four hundred miles from Mesilla."

Alex smiled. "Well, all I've got to say is, ole Billy

the Kid must have had him a mustang that could run like Breathtaker."

As the truck rolled into Ruidoso city limits, there were various businesses along the road. There were antiques and wood carvings advertised for sale that sat out near the road. Then, off to the right down several hundred feet below lay the race track. The white rails and the well-groomed track could be seen clearly and in the background the luxurious grandstand stood tall. The barns that housed the many stalls lay to the east of the grandstand. Jess slowed the Ford and turned into the drive leading down to the facility. At the entrance, there was a rather large impressive sculptured artwork of horses running and frolicking with their nostrils flaring and manes flowing in the wind.

Susan was all eyes. "Jess, this is it! This is where we make it or break it. I guess we've been waiting ten years to have a horse good enough to come here for this race."

"Well, Susan, we've done everything *we* can do. Now it's up to that gray devil back there in that red trailer to do the rest. Alex has him in top shape, so make no mistake, girl, he'll be in there battling for the lead when race day comes."

After they had unloaded Breathtaker and all the gear, Alex dipped up a feeding of grain, carried it into Breathtaker's stall and poured it in his trough. He stood talking to him for a second. "Ole boy, it has been a long time since breakfast, hasn't it? I knew you were ready for your grain and alfalfa wasn't you, boy? You're tired from all that riding but you can rest all day tomorrow." Alex slid his hand down Breathtaker's neck, petted him lightly, and then stepped out the stall door.

Jess walked up about that time with a chain and padlock. "Here, Alex, take this chain and lock the stall door and then we'll go eat and check in at the motel."

"Jess, I'm staying here. Remember,"

"I know, but after we pick up the rental car, you can have the truck to come back."

Alex hesitated a second. "Okay, I'll be back over here in an hour probably."

Chapter 26

The next few days were filled with work, grooming and exercising Breathtaker. It was the day before the trial races and Alex had worked Breathtaker on the track a couple of times the week before and he was in top form. In all the coffee shops and restaurants around town, the talk was of the upcoming trial races and predictions as to who would win and make the Derby. Jess and Susan paid close attention to the gossip regarding the races but not once had they heard a word about Breathtaker. The conversations that they had overheard seemed to center around five horses. There was a horse called 'Dash For The Wind' that was a favorite to make the cut. There was 'Gold Coast Money,' 'Jet Fuel, 'Tiptoethroughthecash,' then a horse named, 'East Coast Express' was being talked about quite often. Alex had drawn the three hole in the second heat and was pleased with the position. About two o'clock Jess walked into the barn and Alex was lying on his cot resting. "You awake, Alex?"

Alex sat up on the side of the cot. "Sit down, Jess, get the weight off of your feet."

Jess sat down on the side of the cot. "Alex, I have not heard a word about Breathtaker since we got here. It's as if he doesn't exist."

Alex laughed. "Yeah, makes me feel just like a thief. What they don't know is that big gray devil back there in the stall is about to rob them."

"I sure hope you're right. It seems to me that there would be some mention of him, by some one."

Alex looked down the shed row in both directions to assure no one was watching and then he pulled out his wallet. "Jess, tomorrow, I'll be busy before the race. Give these two one- hundred-dollar bills to Susan and tell her to buy 2 *win* tickets on number 3 in the second race. I don't gamble much unless I feel like it's a sure thing."

"Sure, Alex, but what if the odds are high, do you still want her to bet it all?"

"Absolutely, the odds don't have a thing to do with Breathtaker's ability. They just don't know what he is and what he can do. They are ignoring him completely. Jess, you're thinking about winning this race just like me. Jess, I'm an opportunist and I'm interested in a fat bonus as well to go along with the win percentage."

Jess and Susan were up at 6:30 and ready to go to the coffee shop. "Here Susan, Alex wanted you to buy him two one-hundred-dollar win tickets on number three in the second race."

"Jess, that's Breathtaker! No one thinks he can win."

"Alex does. So buy them for him."

As they entered the coffee shop the house was packed with racing fans. There was a constant rumble of conversation regarding the day of racing. Jess purchased a racing form at the check-out counter and quickly turned to the second race. "Look, they've got him picked at dead last with starting odds at 60 to 1."

"Jess, do you think he can win?"

"I know he can win and so does Alex. Breathtaker don't know anything about those odds and he can run with the best of them. He's already proven that in the Black Gold trials."

They finished their coffee. Neither of them wanted

anything to eat, especially on a day of racing like this one about to begin.

It was now 2:30 and post time for the second race. Jess and Susan didn't go to the saddling paddock this time. They went to the betting window. Jess waited while Susan purchased Alex's tickets then they walked out to the rail. Jess took a look at the totals board in the infield and the odds remained the same number three was at 60 to 1.

Jess looked at the racing form again. "Look Susan, two of the horses we've heard so much about are in this race. There's East Coast Express in No 1 position and in fifth position is Gold Coast Money."

Susan looked at the totals board. "East Coast Express is at 3 to 1 and Gold Cost Money is 2 to 1."

Suddenly the air was shattered with the call of boots and saddles and the horses began to come out onto the track. East Coast Express was a big coal black speedster that pranced and frothed at the mouth, ready to run. Next was Breathtaker. He pranced and tossed his head as if to say yes. He was a good-looking race horse, thought Jess. The number three horse was a palomino-colored colt that danced crossways as he was led along. Number four was a fast-looking sorrel with two back stocking legs. He danced proudly with his mane flowing in the wind. Number five was a somewhat short horse but demonstrated powerful muscles and he was ready to run. Number 6 was a horse called "Extended Effort' and he was frothing at the mouth with a light nervous sweat on his neck. Number seven was a calm sorrel that seemed to take every thing in stride. Number eight danced and chomped at the bit, ready to run. Number nine was a black with one sock foot on the back. He was a fine looking race horse and ready. And number ten was a gray not as large as Breathtaker but demonstrating good racing lines. As they rounded the far turn, Breathtaker frolicked and kicked out and Jess knew that he was playing just as he had done on the trail in

Mexico.

"Look at him, Susan, he's really feeling good. Somebody's about to get a surprise, I think."

"Jess, if he wins and afterwards the Derby, let's not run him anymore. Let's just ride him and use him as our herd stallion."

"Agreed," said Jess.

They were now beginning to enter the starting gate. The first eight horses all walked in easily. Number nine and ten were giving trouble but slowly and surely they went inside the gate.

There was a brief pause. A calm stillness lay across the multitude of people at the track. Jess could see through the binoculars that Breathtaker had already crouched down for the start. Suddenly the gates flew open and a thunder of hooves shattered the air and the crowd went wild.

The Announcer voice came over the loud speaker, *"It's Gold Coast Money in the lead and number six Extended Effort challenging. Number four East Cost Express coming up fast. Number three, Breathtaker holding his own on the outside of the group. As they come to the half way point, it's Breathtaker driving hard on the outside but Gold Coast Money holding on to the lead. Oh, my folks, it's Breathtaker taking the lead and coming fast. He's out front by two lengths and Gold Coast Money falls back to the third position. Here comes Extended Effort making a bid, he's challenging Breathtaker a length behind on the outside. As they dash under the wire it's Breathtaker by two lengths, Extended Effort second and Gold Coast Money third. Who would have ever thought that possible?"*

Jess grabbed Susan, lifted her completely off the ground and swung her around about three times then shouted at the top of his lungs. "Winners circle girl. It's photograph time in New Mexico!"

By the time they got to the winners circle Alex was

already there. He was excited. When he saw Jess and Susan he shouted. "I told you!!! I knew it!!! I knew it!!! I knew he was the best! Ye Hoo…"

After the picture was taken, Alex led Breathtaker off to the test barn. Susan turned to Jess. "Let's go collect our wagers."

"You mean Alex's wagers."

"No, I mean ours, too. Here's one for you. She handed Jess a hundred dollar *win* ticket she had purchased. Then she looked up at Jess and smiled sweetly. "I've got one, too," she said.

Jess stood with his mouth open, smiling, but shocked. He would never have dreamed that Susan believed that strongly in Breathtaker being able to win after what she had said that morning in the coffee shop.

Chapter 27

Alex got his money from the win ticket, all $10,720.00 of it, and he was floating on cloud nine. Jess walked into the barn the following day after the race and Alex was busy with a pen scratching on a pad.

Jess cast a questioning look at Alex. "What are you doing, Alex, counting your money?"

"I was just figuring how many good, double "A" mares I could buy to breed to Breathtaker. Jess, I want to pay you right now for the stud fees. How much are you going to charge for introductory breeding fee?"

"Well . . . To you, Alex, when Breathtaker is a three year old, I'll breed a limit of two mares for say $1.00 each. How is that?"

Alex looked at Jess with a blank stare on his face. "Hells fire yes! Here's my booking fees right here and I'm writing it down," as he scrambled for the two dollars.

"The reason I say that, Alex, is if we win the Derby, I am only going to breed Tony's mares and yours. The book will be closed on Breathtaker. I'll breed only my own mares then if people want one of his foals, it will cost plenty."

As the days passed before the up-coming All-American Derby, Alex worked Breathtaker a couple of times at the track just to get the kinks out and keep him in shape. He didn't want to take a lot of edge off him, he wanted him to be a little high, feel fresh and be ready to run like the wind come race day.

Jess and Susan did quite a bit of shopping and looking around as they waited for the up-coming big race. Jess was fascinated by one of the local landmarks. It was an old mill down in the village of Ruidoso. The old mill had been purchased and turned into a museum sometime during the mid-twentieth century. Over in one corner of the rather large room there was a grinding stone turning slowly, powered by the waterwheel. The curator and owner, was a very nice lady and she explained in depth to Jess how it all operated. The water wheel operated the small grinding stone and the stone ground small portions of flour that she sacked for sale to the tourists. Jess stood watching the stone slowly grind the flour and instantly he knew there was too much old west history associated with that mill for him not to have a bag of that brown flour.

It was 1:00 P.M. September first when Jess and Susan Steel stood at the saddling paddock, leaning against the rail watching the finalists for the All-American Derby. There was a field of twelve of the country's best young race horses preparing to run for the richest Quarter Horse Race in the word. The purse would be in excess of a million dollars to the winner. The successful young speedster would receive prestigious notoriety that would go down in the racing records as one of the world's best.

Alex had lucked out at the drawing and had drawn the inside position. Alex liked the inside spot. He believed there was advantage there whether there actually was or not. Breathtaker stood calmly while Jess placed the small pancake racing saddle on his back and tightened the girth. Alex stood stroking Breathtaker's neck, talking to him. Breathtaker nibbled lightly at Alex's shoulder as if to say, calm down Alex, it's all in a days work. He seemed to know that he had a job to do and that job wasn't to walk the circle that day, it was run and run like he had never run before in his young life. He was running against the best. They were the elite, the caliber that made few mistakes, for they were excellent and the pick of the futurity lot and the best in the world.

As Jess stood looking at the horses, he knew that some of the colts had been flown in from other parts of the country. Some had been hauled to Ruidoso in fifty or sixty thousand dollar trailers or maybe even more expensive vans. Many of the colts were owned by rich men, syndications or limited partnerships. Jess also knew there was one that rode 835 miles in a $ 3,000.00 used, three-horse slant trailer in need of paint and he was owned by an Oklahoma cowboy with very little money. But that day it didn't matter because one looked as good as the other, for they were all good. Jess thought about it for a second longer, realizing that Alex Haygood wasn't a rich trainer with a big reputation like some of the others, but he knew as much about a racehorse as any man in the world and the All American was no strange place to him.

Jess looked at Susan and noticed that her eyes were moist. Jess squeezed her hand and then leaned down and kissed her on the cheek. "It will be okay, whether we win or loose. At least we made it here and that is something that 99% of the owners and trainers never get to experience in a whole lifetime."

"Oh, I was just thinking about Breathtaker. He raced to help you catch a killer in the Mexican desert. Now today he's trying to help us win a million dollars. That's almost too much to ask of him."

Jess thought about what Susan had said. "Well, Susan, he's doing what he was bred and trained to do. When I was trying to get him to breathe by blowing in his little lungs the morning he was born I had a feeling that this day would come. He was a very special foal because he was a fighter and he'll be a fighter today."

The crisp sound of the trumpeter's 'boots and saddles' rang out clearly in the New Mexico air and Alex legged the jockey into the saddle. "Jackie, I don't have to tell you how to ride him, just do it . . . and good luck to us all."

Jess and Susan dashed out of the saddling paddock area and headed for the rail. They squirmed their way up to the rail and watched the horses as they paraded by. Breathtaker was the best looking horse on the track as far a Susan was concerned. He carried his head high with his dark main and tail flowing in the New Mexico breeze. Jackie spotted Jess and Susan standing by the rail and smiled and tipped his cap as he passed by. They watched as one by one the horses turned and started around the track. Breathtaker jogged for a few strides and then fell into a short canter with long sleek neck arched as he pulled on the bit. As they reached the back stretch, Jess saw Breathtaker do his usual frolicking and playing.

"Susan, look at him - he's feeling good out there."

Susan reached in her purse and came out with a bottle of medication. "Here, swallow one of these pills. I got them from the doctor a few days before we left home. He said it would settle our nerves and for us to take one, five minutes before the race."

"Good," said Jess, as he threw the pill in his mouth and swallowed.

As the horses neared the starting gate, Jess lifted the binoculars and watched the horses enter. Breathtaker stepped quietly into the gate and then one by one the others followed suit. There were commotions in the gates. The crowd grew silent for what seemed like thirty seconds.

And the voice rang out. . .

"They're off. . ." "It's 'Breathtaker' making a fast start along the rail and 'String of Pearls second'. 'Dash for the Money' looks to be third... My, Oh My... It's just too close to call and a three horse race it is . . . . Now 'Dash for the Money' making his bid and now in front by a nose. 'String of Pearls' running second now as 'Breathtaker' falls back. It's 'Dash for the money' and 'String of Pearls'

as they battle for the lead... Wait . . . Wait . . . There's movement on the inside next to the rail. It's 'Breathtaker' charging hard. He's really turning it on as they reach the half way mark. Here he comes, folks, it's 'Breathtaker' now firing on all cylinders as he takes the lead. It's 'Breathtaker' by a length now. Look- at- him- fly . . . Folks did you ever see anything like that? As they near the wire, It is all 'Breathtaker' today . . . As they sweep under the wire. It's 'Breathtaker' winning by an impressive three lengths, 'String of Pearls' second and 'Dash for the Money' third. What- a -horse race. This Oklahoma colt can fly . . . my, my, my . . . And there you have it, the winner of the All American Derby. A gray horse called 'Breathtaker' owned by Jess and Susan Steele is the undisputed winner. From out of nowhere they came with their gray colt and their dreams. From a little town in Oklahoma to a little town in New Mexico they brought this wonderful horse and they have taken –it –all- today."

Jess grabbed Susan and kissed her. Both of them were overcome with joy and crying.

"He's the best in the world, Susan! Breathtaker is the best in the world and he'll never have to run again," shouted Jess.

They made it to the winners circle and Alex was beside himself. "We did it!!! We did it, Jess," shouted Alex, at the top of his lungs.

Breathtaker pranced nervously as they placed the floral wreath on his sleek neck. Jess, Susan and Alex stood along side Breathtaker holding the fancy red cooler with the All American logo.

Alex looked at each of them. "I want us to all enjoy this win, it will never happen to us again in this lifetime."

As soon as the press finished the picture session, Alex led Breathtaker off toward the test barn.

It was Sunday morning and the day after the big win

when Alex and Jess drove up in front of the barn at Ruidoso Downs. As they entered the barn, Alex walked straight to Breathtaker's stall and stepped inside.

"Jess . . . Come quick we've got a problem," shouted Alex.

Jess ran to the stall and as he walked in, he could see that Breathtaker was holding his right front foot up off the stall floor. Jess swore quietly to himself. Alex began examining the foot and leg but could not find a problem.

"I'll call the vet," said Jess, as he dashed out of the stall and to the barn telephone that hung on the wall by the tack room door.

An hour later the Veterinarian kneeled down and carefully examined Breathtaker's leg. Finding nothing obvious, he took several field X-Rays and then asked his assistant to take them back to the office and develop the film. "Hurry back," he said as he quietly continued to examine the sore leg for a while. He stood up then turned to Jess and Alex. "The problem seems to be in the shoulder but I can't be sure until we get the film back. Have you got a lamp or something that we can hold the film up to look at it?"

Alex picked up his battery lantern. "I've got this lantern, will it work?"

"That will work fine."

"He may have just sprained his shoulder, at least that's what we hope has happened. He's sure a beautiful horse and he is the fastest horse I've ever seen run. I'm sure he has actually run so hard until he has hurt himself."

An hour later the veterinarian stood holding the film up to the lantern. "Well, it's not good but it could be much worse,"

"What's the problem?" asked Jess.

"Look right here, see that thin line, it's not very long but that's a slight fracture along the front side of the shoulder blade. Mr. Steel, I'll put it to you straight. He will recover with proper care but it's not likely that he will ever compete again," he said, with a troubled look on his face.

There was a long silence as Jess looked down at the stall floor and stood quietly for a little while. Jess looked over at Alex. Jess could see that Alex's eyes were moist and a single tear trickle down the weathered face of the little man and Jess knew he was hurting.

Alex shook his head and looked at Jess. "Well, Jess, I guess we pushed him too hard."

"Alex, Breathtaker is a race horse and he's the best racehorse in the world. He runs because he likes it. You know you have never had to hit him or lay the crop on him to get him to run."

Alex seemed to find some strength in what Jess had said. "What do we do for him, Doc?"

"Well, I'm going to put him on Banamine and a little Phenylbutazone for a few days until the pain subsides. We'll also start him on antibiotics. There will likely be some swelling so get prepared for that. I'd keep him here few weeks. If everything goes well for the next 30 days, then get back to Oklahoma, turn him out on pasture for the rest of the summer and fall. Mr. Steele, the best veterinarian and healer on earth is old Mother Nature. She has a way of healing animals like this. Just turn him out and let him be a horse for a while just like God intended. Have an X-Ray done again in a few months and take a look see. If everything heals like I expect it to, you can ride him all you want but I wouldn't advise racing him."

Jess walked out of the barn with the veterinarian. "Well, I plan to use him as a breeding stallion, so it's not a loss. Doc, that being said, there's no one earth that knows how much I hate this for Alex's sake." Jess then turned and looked back through the door down the shed row. Jess knew that Alex was blaming himself.

"Jess, it could have been much worse, I've had to

put seven colts down already this year. They were good colts, too, all with broken legs," said the vet. He cranked his truck and backed out of the drive.

The next few weeks were filled with caring for Breathtaker. Susan came to the barn everyday and would hold a heating pad on his shoulder for a full hour morning and night. Alex and Jess kept up the medication just as they had been instructed. After 30 days the swelling had left the shoulder and there was no pain so they loaded Breathtaker and they went back to Oklahoma.

Alex turned Breathtaker out for the rest of the summer and fall. Jess was busy working at buying mares for Tony and he had found three. With the three that Jess had decided to sell that made a total of six good brood mares with which Tony could start a herd.

Jess had been in regular contact with Tony over the past few weeks, discussing Breathtaker winning the All American and Tony's new venture. Tony had learned about Breathtaker's unfortunate accident and had expressed his deepest sympathy. He had also told Jess that they were pleasantly surprised to learn that Emanuel and Teresa's child would be born in the spring. Tony was absolutely beside himself concerning the upcoming event, especially since they had learned that it was going to be a boy.

It was late November now and Breathtaker had continued to mend. Both Jess and Alex watched his movements closely. He would run and kick up his heels as though nothing has ever happened.

Jess walked in the barn just as Alex finished his chores. They sat drinking a cup of coffee and then Alex looked over at Jess. "Let's take Breathtaker in to the vet's office and have him X-Rayed this afternoon."

"Sounds like a good idea, I'm about ready to ride a good horse for a change. That is, if the vet says it's all right."

The veterinarian studied the X-Ray for a long time

and after he had finished, he turned to Jess. "Jess, I can't see the slightest trace of the fracture from any direction. I do believe Breathtaker has completely healed and if you want to ride him, well, I'd say to just have at it,"

Jess smiled, "Thanks Doc, I'll do just that. Oh, by the way, I want to pasture breed six mares to him come early spring. You think if I turn him in with them there will that be a problem with his shoulder?"

"Not at all. He'll stay out of their way. Those old mares have a way of providing a quick education for a young stallion. He's smart and he'll know in about five minutes when to stay away from the girls and when not too."

Jess winked at the doc. "Took ole Alex ten years to figure that one out," said Jess, as he busted out laughing. Alex smiled, then his ears turned a bright red and Jess knew that he was a little bit embarrassed. Jess also knew that Alex didn't mind him picking at him that way.

Chapter 28

It was the first week in March now and the cold wind howled and bit at the corner of the barn. A late winter storm was in the forecast and the sustained winds came directly out of the north all afternoon. Alex had put all of the colts in the barn for the night, but Breathtaker didn't bring up his mares and that worried Alex a little.

"Jess, you think we need to go look for Breathtaker and his girls?"

"I guess he knows what he's doing. Maybe it won't snow and if it does we'll look first thing in the morning."

Jess awoke at six o'clock and a heavy snow had fallen during the night. He finished his coffee then went to the mud room and began pulling his insulated Carhartts on over his jeans.

Susan walked in about that time and cast a questioning look at Jess. "Where are you off to?"

"Oh, I figured I'd walk back in the pasture and see if I can find Breathtaker and his mares. He didn't bring them up yesterday afternoon."

"You be careful back there and watch for falling limbs if you get into the timber. They will be heavy from the snow."

"Oh, I will."

Jess hung over his shoulder the halter and lead rope he had brought to the house the evening before and headed out toward the back of the pasture. There was a good twelve inches of snow on the ground and for Oklahoma that was a big snow. After he had gone about a half mile, he came upon a deep snow drift at the end of a meadow that ran east to west along the creek. There was a gap in the timber that created a kind of wind tunnel that had caused the snow to drift. He had seen no sign of the horses so he went on. The snow had stuck to the north side of the trees, creating a flocking of winter wonder like he had seen on Christmas cards. There had evidently been freezing rain before the snow hit for icicles hung long from an outcropping of rock a quarter mile south of the deep drift. Big Sallisaw Creek had frozen over, allowing him to cross over on the thick ice. Jess crawled up the far bank and stood listening and looking far into the timber for any sign of movement. Three hundred yards away he made out the image of three white tail deer slipping through the brush. Jess knew that it was likely they had seen him when he came up out of the creek. Suddenly, three wild turkeys flew out of a big red oak above him and sailed above the tree tops to the south. Jess eased on, keeping close to the creek as he continued to look for Breathtaker and his mares. He knew they would be bunched up somewhere in order to protect themselves from the bitter wind. As Jess moved on, he thought about his grandfather and how he had been out tracking livestock in a deep snow the day he died. The old man had been out for several hours trying to find some of his hogs that ran loose on free range down in the big timber country of south Arkansas. The old man had returned from his search, stomped the snow off his feet and come into his pa's house to get warm. He had tied sacks to his feet to keep them warm and still had them on with his feet propped up on the fireplace hearth, in an effort to warm them. Jess's pa began to talk to him but he didn't answer so his pa thought he had fallen asleep. After sitting there for an hour or more, Jess's Pa tried to wake him up and found that he had died there peacefully by the fire.

It was getting on toward noon when Jess dropped

off into a wide draw that covered about fifteen acres. There was a stand of big red oak timber that grew down in and along the side of the draw. Jess remembered from hunting back in the area there was a long outcropping of rock to the north side down near the end of the draw. There was a ledge of rock that hung out over the bank in some places twenty feet or more creating a shelter that he had used to get out of the rain once. As Jess stepped out from behind a big red oak, he looked toward the outcropping and saw movement in the distance. Sure enough about three hundred yards down the draw there were the horses bunched under the rock ledge. Breathtaker came out of the herd and began to rear, pawing the air viciously, tossing his head and screaming as Jess moved closer.

"That's strange. He's never acted like this before," said Jess, as he talked to himself. Jess moved closer and Breathtaker continued to act suspiciously defensive toward him. Jess eased on up closer and was now within fifty or sixty feet of him and he continued to rear and paw the air. Suddenly Jess's heart seemed to skip a beat and cold fear gripped him down to the bottom of his cold feet. From that distance Jess could now see what looked to be large splotches of blood on his sides. His front legs were all scratched up and Jess knew the stallion had been in trouble. Jess swore quietly. "Damn it, he's been tangled in wire." Jess continued moving closer, trying to get a better look. Breathtaker continued to rear and paw the air viciously, bunching his mares in an even tighter circle. Something is wrong here, thought Jess. He scanned the area out away from the horses carefully and then suddenly he could see an area that looked to be fifty feet wide where the snow had been torn up and trampled. Jess could see splotches of blood around the area in the snow. Jess made his way on toward the area and as he approached he saw the problem. There lying in the middle of the area was a hundred-and-seventy-five pound cougar and he was dead. He had been torn to shreds by Breathtaker's pounding hoofs and vicious teeth. It had been a fight to the finish and Breathtaker had killed his attacker in an attempt to defend his ladies.

Jess continued to talk to Breathtaker as he made his way closer and under the edge of the shelter. Jess eased his hand in his pocket and took out a cube of sugar and slowly held it out toward the young stallion. Even though Breathtaker knew Jess's familiar voice, he was still fired up and ready to give more battle to protect his girls and Jess knew it. Suddenly Breathtaker smelled the sugar and moved forward toward Jess a little, stretched his long, arched neck forward and took the sugar out of Jess's hand. Jess continued to ease forward while continuing to talk to him then offered him another cube. Jess eased the halter over Breathtaker's nose and buckled it over the head then attached the lead rope.

As Jess led Breathtaker out from under the ledge, the mares followed reluctantly and Breathtaker never missed an opportunity to call them as he pranced in the deep snow. The claw marks on his legs were many but they didn't appear to be severe. Jess knew that a few days of care and with the application of Alex's magic ointment, they would be healed.

It took almost three hours in the deep snow to make their way up and around the head of the frozen creek. Once they were around, they headed straight for the barn. It was cold as they headed into the bitter north wind and it burned and cut at Jess's face. Jess suddenly thought about crossing the hot, dusty, desert down in Mexico and wasn't sure but what the heat was better. As they came up to the barn, Jess opened the pasture gate and led Breathtaker into the barn and put him into his freshly bedded stall. The mares were all bunched near the gate so Jess just opened the gate and let them all run into the shed row. After closing the sliding door at the end of the barn he caught the mares one by one and fastened them in warm, dry stalls.

Jess was just putting the last mare in a stall when Alex walked into the barn. He had needed to run an errand and had told Jess that he would be late for work.

"I see you found them," said Alex.

"And, boy was it ever cold. Breathtaker's got a few scratches and cuts that we need to take care of but he's all right," said Jess, as he hung the halter and lead rope in the tack room.

Alex hurried to Breathtaker's stall and stepped inside. "What the hell? What happened to him Jess? Wire?"

"A cat. A big cat. The cat tried to get at the mares sometime early this morning and Breathtaker took the battle to him. It was a fight to the finish. Alex, they met each other out in the open woods some fifty yards from where the mares were bunched under that big rock ledge that lays back to the south. It looked as though they got down to business and fought for maybe an hour or more according to the signs. When I walked up to where they had fought, there was an area about fifty feet wide. The ground was all torn up and there was blood everywhere. Then I spotted the cat lying out near the middle of the area. He was a big cougar, at least what was left of him. Alex, Breathtaker had absolutely torn that cat to pieces. It must have been some battle, because Breathtaker was still full of fight, didn't even want me to get my hands on him and he didn't mind showing it a bit."

Over the next few days Alex doctored Breathtaker religiously and the scratches were all healed and he was as good as ever. The spring rains had begun and yellow jonquils were blooming at the entrance to the barn and new foals were being born. It was a busy time around the barn during the foaling season but Jess knew that he must deliver Tony's mares to him. They were all safely in foal now and he had talked to Tony on the telephone a few days back. Tony was excited. He had a healthy new grandson and he had completed his barn and was ready to receive the mares whenever time permitted. Arrangements had been made for Alex to deliver the mares and plans had been made for Tony to meet Alex just beyond the point of entry and direct him to the farm. Jess was also excited about Tony's new venture and knew that Tony would do well with the quality brood mares that were now in foal to Breathtaker.

Chapter 29

Twelve seasons had passed since Tony begun to raise horses and he had done well. There were some things around Jess and Susan's ranch that inevitably had changed over the years. One change dealt Jess and Susan a powerful blow. Alex had experienced a heart attack and passed away two years earlier, and Jess had never quite gotten over the loss of his true friend.

Breathtaker was now fourteen and had proven himself one of the leading sires in the country. Jess had retired from racing and was involved in breeding and raising a few quality foals each year. He had also become interested in the Registered Texas Longhorn breed of cattle and had purchased a small herd of Longhorns to keep him busy. Susan was still just as attentive and as pretty she had always been. Jess and Susan enjoyed riding the pastures frequently. Susan had fallen in love with Breathtaker and she and Jess took turns riding him. They would take long rides back into the pasture and Susan would carry a picnic lunch. Sometime they would sit for hours just talking and watching the deer and the other wild creatures they had come to know. Jess, of course, had aged a little, just as Breathtaker had, but the bond between him and the big gray stallion had only grown stronger with each passing year. Tony had done well with his horses and every Christmas Jess and Susan received beautiful cards with pictures of his horses on them.

It was early spring now and it was just getting gray

light in the east when Jess finished saddling Breathtaker. The sparrows were coming off their roost and the shed row was littered with straw from their frantic nest building. A momma cat had arrived at the barn a few months earlier and she had delivered a litter of fuzzy kittens in the back corner of the tack room. They were big enough to play now and they were busy with a game of roll and tumble at Breathtaker's feet. It seemed that he knew they were there, for he would ease his feet around ever so slowly to avoid stepping on them. Jess stood and watched them play for a little while and then led Breathtaker out of the barn, stepped in the stirrup and mounted up. Susan wasn't feeling well that day so he decided to ride alone to try and savor his favorite part of the day back in the timber country.

As they rode away from the barn Breathtaker demonstrated his usual prancing and show off disposition, flaunting his masculine beauty to five brood mares that stood at the fence in the next pasture. Jess chuckled quietly and petted the stallion on the neck.

"You never miss an opportunity to flirt, do you, boy?"

Jess nudged Breathtaker with is right boot and they moved on down the trail that led to the woods.

After they had entered the woods and arrived at the favorite place of peaceful tranquility that he enjoyed so much, Jess drew up and quietly dismounted. He tied the reins to a small bush and sat down on his favorite log, looking far out across the draw. In the distance some three hundred yards away, he saw a doe with two yearling fawns standing looking at him and noticed that Breathtaker was looking directly at them with his ears pricked forward. Two squirrels were scampering in the canopy above, playing a game of reproductive tag, just as he had seen squirrels do so many seasons in the past. Jess placed his hands to his mouth and made the call of an owl and far off down the creek he heard the answer of a wild gobbler quickly challenging any wise old owl that would infringe on his territory.

    Somewhere in Mexico, a dove called from far out in a canyon and a coyote lay on the side of a sand dune, at the mouth of her den, nursing her three young pups. An eagle soared high above the sheer walls of the canyon with graceful ease, floating on the currents above the peaks, and a thousand feet below, the sun-bleached bones of two killers lay decaying, slowly processing into dust. Two old horses, a sorrel and a bay, grazed on the canyon floor not far away from the bones, nipping the tender shoots of spring grass that they must share to survive. The purple sage that dotted the canyon floor swayed gently to the spring breeze and yellow wild flowers had sprung forth dotting the landscape with color. The breath of the devil breathed ghostly through the narrow mouth of the canyon and the leaves of the cottonwood whispered gently from high above. A hundred fifty miles away, far down in the Rio Grande valley a dark foal lay momentarily motionless on the soft bedded floor of a foaling stall. The young hands of a Mexican boy were gently drying the foal's face with a hand towel as his grandfather stood watching him. The dark foal was a beauty and no doubt would become a gray like his grandsire. As the young boy gently stroked the face of the foal a magical transformation was taking shape. A feeling of irreversible love for a horse was being planted deep in the boy's heart and mind. A feeling that would grow and one that would last forever. Yes, it would be a very special bond, a bond between a boy and a beautiful gray horse that he would call - Toma Suspiro Dos. Breathtaker Two.

THE END